Those who knew her best had never had a clue how much Anna had longed for a child.

It was a cruel stroke of fate that had ended that hope years ago. But she had her career.

Her career!

"I can't be pregnant." The room seemed to swirl around. She closed her eyes against the dizziness.

Tanner! Oh, God. He would kill her when he found out. She had told him there was no danger of her getting pregnant. She had told him not to worry; she couldn't have a baby. How could this happen?

She was pregnant by her new boss...and now she had to tell him!

Barbara McMahon was born and raised
in the southern United States, but settled in
California after spending a year flying around the
world for an international airline. After settling
down to raise a family and work for a computer
firm, she began writing when her children started
school. Now, feeling fortunate in having realized
a long-held dream of quitting her day job and
writing full-time, she has moved with her husband
to the Sierra Nevada mountains of California,
where she finds her desire to write is stronger
than ever. With the beauty of the mountains
visible from her windows, and the pace of life
slower than that of the hectic San Francisco Bay
Area, where they previously resided, she finds more
time than ever to think up stories and characters
and share them with others through writing.
Barbara loves to hear from readers. You can reach
her at P.O. Box 977, Pioneer, CA 95666-0977,
U.S.A., and readers can also contact Barbara at
her Web site: www.barbaramcmahon.com.

BARBARA MCMAHON
The Boss's Little Miracle

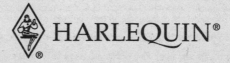

TORONTO • NEW YORK • LONDON
AMSTERDAM • PARIS • SYDNEY • HAMBURG
STOCKHOLM • ATHENS • TOKYO • MILAN • MADRID
PRAGUE • WARSAW • BUDAPEST • AUCKLAND

ISBN-13: 978-0-373-18339-5
ISBN-10:   0-373-18339-9

THE BOSS'S LITTLE MIRACLE

First North American Publication 2007.

www.eHarlequin.com

Printed in U.S.A.

*If you want to escape the winter
and jet off to the intense, balmy heat of the
desert—then make a date with Barbara McMahon
next year!*

Rescued by the Sheikh

*When photographer Lisa Sullinger got stuck in the desert, the
last thing she expected was to be rescued by a sheikh! Lisa
can't help but fall for brooding Tuareg al Shaldor.... Is there
a place for an ordinary girl like her in his guarded heart?*

On sale February 2007, only from Harlequin Romance®!

To Ruth Johnson,
May all your travels be happy events,
and may you have books galore to read.

CHAPTER ONE

ANNA LARKIN came out of the underground station into the pouring rain. The gusting wind made using an umbrella impossible. She bent her head and began walking up Montgomery Street. Her cross trainers were getting wet, but better than soaking the high heels, which she carried in her tote bag. Her hair would be a mess, curls everywhere. But not to be helped, it was the least of her worries.

San Francisco was often rainy in late October and today was no exception.

She just wished it had been sunny—or at least dry. She was coming down with the flu. Walking in the rain would certainly do nothing to help. Bad things came in threes, she mused. First her sister's call this weekend to jubilantly share the news she was expecting a new baby. Anna had tried to rejoice with her sister, but without the chance of having a baby herself, each time she had to pretend it didn't matter it got harder.

Then—the flu. She was usually healthy rarely even getting a cold during the winter. She so did not need this.

Now hurrying through the rain to get to work in order to meet the new man who was taking charge of the company today was about the last straw. All she wanted to do was curl up in bed and sleep.

She reached the cavernous lobby of the high-rise building in short order. Entering, she shook as much of the water as she could from her raincoat and hair before getting on one of the express elevators. She hoped there was time to dry her hair before the meeting. The natural curls always dominated in damp weather.

She no sooner stepped off on her floor than her colleague, and friend, Teresa accosted her.

"You look terrible," she said, grabbing Anna's arm and hurrying her along to the ladies' room. Once safely inside, Anna peered at her reflection in the mirror. She looked worse than she felt, if that was possible. Pale with wet hanks of hair framing her face, she looked like she had the flu.

"Today's the day we finally meet the new boss, you're certain to make an impression," Teresa teased. "Hurry up. He's called for a meeting of department heads at nine."

"I feel sick as a dog," Anna said, slipping off her

cross trainers. "I think it's the flu. I've been sick all weekend and wouldn't have come in today if the new CEO wasn't starting. Just when I need to make a good impression if I want that promotion."

"I thought Mr. Taylor said it was in the bag," said Teresa, holding the tote and reaching for Anna's high heels.

The rain had left her stockings wet, but they would dry soon enough. She took the offered heels, tossing her wet raincoat over one of the stall doors, letting it drip onto the tile floor. Better here than in her office.

Once she was standing in the shoes, she took her comb from her bag and began to pull it through her hair confining the unruly curls as best she could, anchoring them at her nape. This was not the way she normally wore it but a riot of damp curls was not going to win her any points with the new boss. What else could go wrong today?

Teresa checked her watch. "We have five minutes to get into the conference room," she said. "I'm not going to be late to the first meeting he's called."

Anna checked one more time in the mirror. She looked as professional as she could given the circumstances. She pinched her cheeks to get some color into her face, double-checked her lipstick and turned to her friend. "I'm as ready as I'll ever be."

Walking down the long hall she felt the suppressed excitement. Everyone on the floor knew Mr. Taylor was retiring. The Board of Directors had selected a new chief executive officer—but kept all information quiet lest the competition heard about it before they were ready with their announcement. Even the top level of management of Drysdale Electronics didn't know who would be the new CEO.

Rumors had abounded over the last few weeks that he would make a clean sweep of the current managers and directors and bring in his own people. Of course that kind of rumor went around every time a new man took charge. Sometimes it was even true.

In passing the employee's lounge, Anna dashed in to get a cup of coffee. She had not felt up to eating anything for breakfast so needed a jolt of caffeine to keep going. If at all possible, once the initial meeting was finished, she would go home and crawl back into bed. She was rarely sick and couldn't remember the last time she'd felt so wonky.

Entering the conference room a couple of moments later she immediately looked at the head of the room. Allen Taylor was talking with a man who had his back toward the gathering. The new CEO obviously. She couldn't tell much from that view—he was tall, had dark hair with no gray in it and a wide set of shoulders. For a moment she thought there was something familiar about him. But no one even knew the name of the new man, the secrecy surrounding his appointment has been tightly capped.

He obviously wasn't as old as Mr. Taylor, not if that black hair was any indication.

Anna glanced around, recognizing all the senior management of the home office. Slipping into the seat next to Teresa, she sipped the warm coffee, wishing she was still in bed. How long was this going to take?

Glancing around at the others, she picked up on the tension in the room. She knew they all had questions and concerns.

After her conversation with Mr. Taylor last Friday, however, she wasn't as nervous as she might have been. He had assured her that her promotion was in the bag. By January she would be in her new position as director of the European marketplace, headquartered in Brussels. She could hardly wait.

Mr. Taylor stepped to the head of the long table as the man beside him turned to face the group. Anna stared at him with stunned, sickening surprise. For a moment heat swept through her and she couldn't tear her gaze away.

He did have broad shoulders; she remembered rubbing her hands over them, feeling the hot skin, the taut muscles. His lips appeared chiseled, but she remembered how they'd molded hers, bringing wild passion to a mere kiss. For three glorious weeks she and Tanner Forsythe had been constantly in each other's company. Two days after they made love, he had stopped calling, stopped returning her calls and dropped out of her life completely.

She swallowed hard. Oh. My. God. She had slept with the new head of Drysdale Electronics!

She felt as if she would throw up. She glanced over at Teresa who was looking at the head of the table with all attention. Nobody knew. She had kept their affair quiet last summer, not wanting to be teased about a whirlwind romance. Thank goodness for discretion. If she could just get through today, she'd make sure nobody ever knew. She had to get to him, make sure he didn't mention anything thinking people might have known about their dating.

Please don't let him say anything, she prayed, wishing she could slink down in her chair, slip beneath the table and hide forever. She had to find a moment to speak to him alone. Assure him no one knew—and no one need ever know.

They'd met when he'd begun coming to the gym where she worked out several times a week. Dressed in running shorts and a T-shirt, he looked fabulous. She'd been instantly drawn to him the first time he'd showed up. Before her session had ended, he'd asked her out for coffee. From then on they'd found time to meet during the week and on the weekends.

She tried to remember all the details of their dates. But her head throbbed and she felt slightly ill again. She so did not need this.

What would this do to a future working relationship? He couldn't fire her outright, could he? She wished she had had some prior inkling of Tanner Forsythe taking on the helm of Drysdale Electronic. What was she going to do?

Mr. Taylor nodded at the group and began to speak, "As you all know, I've talked about retiring for a long time. Mrs. Taylor has finally convinced me to act, not dream. Many of you know the Board met two weeks ago to finalized negotiations with my successor. I spoke with some of you individually last Friday in an attempt to make a smooth transition between my leaving and the assumption of power by our new CEO. I'd like to introduce Tanner Forsythe. He takes over with the full and enthusiastic endorsement of the Board of Directors. He has an impressive background with electronic firms in taking troubled companies and turning them around to make them more profitable than ever. A copy of his impressive résumé is in the packet Ellie will give each of you on the way out. The Board of Directors and I do hope you all will be able to guide Drysdale Electronics to new heights under Tanner's guidance. I expect each of you to give him your full cooperation and support."

Mr. Taylor waited for the polite applause to die down, then nodded to the man on his right. "How about each of you introduce yourself, give the department or division you head up and say anything else you think Tanner may need to know for now. He'll be meeting with each of you individually before the week is out."

Mr. Taylor checked his watch. "However, let's keep it brief, I have a lot to review with him myself before I take off for the Bahamas."

There was some good-natured teasing for a moment. Then Hank Brownson began the introductions with the explanation he ran the accounting department. One by one each person around the table introduced himself or herself and gave a brief description of their area of responsibilities. Teresa's turn came fast. Anna felt sick. She was next. She heard Teresa explain she was the head of Human Resources, then the silence that followed.

Anna looked at Mr. Taylor rather than into the dark familiar eyes of Tanner Forsythe.

"My name is Anna Larkin. I'm the under-director for European operations." She could say nothing further. For one awful moment she wondered if Tanner would rescind the promotion promised and refuse to let her move to the Brussels office.

She had been working toward that particular position for more than ten years. For the last five she'd studied French assiduously. Recently all her vacations had been in Europe to familiarize herself with the different countries, and to practice her language skills. She had devoted fifteen years of her life to becoming the best international marketing employee Drysdale Electronics ever had.

For one heart-stopping moment she wondered if it all had been in vain.

So if bad things came in threes, was this the end? Maybe she'd make a miraculous recovery within the next ten minutes. The news from her sister wouldn't hurt so, and Tanner would send her to Europe with a bonus in her pocket.

And pigs would fly.

As Neil Patterson introduced himself, Anna leaned back in her chair. She had no illusions that life would change in an instant. Her only hope was that she could make it home before collapsing. Looking at the bright side of things, if she were home, he couldn't fire her, could he?

Once introductions were complete, Tanner gave a short speech. Upbeat and direct, he challenged everyone to rise to the new level of expectations. It motivated without casting any aspersions on Mr. Taylor and his stint at the helm. Anna was impressed.

She'd been impressed before—in the summer. They'd spent endless evenings walking around San Francisco after working out together at the gym, enjoying the city when the crowds were gone, and when the weather was at its best. Talking about everything under the sun, or so she thought, he had never mentioned his exact job. And she had only said she was in marketing. She was not defined by her job.

In fact, she'd only talked about it in great detail right before he stopped contacting her.

The penny dropped. He'd known he was being sought for this position and had stopped dating a future employee.

She wished he'd finished things before they'd gone to bed together. Not only for the awkwardness of finding they had to work together, but for the glorious event itself, which would never be repeated. She had begun to fall a little in love with Tanner, even knowing it could lead nowhere. But she'd never found making love to be so exciting, so enthralling as the night they'd spent together.

She kept her gaze on her notepad, her mind drifting to that night, try as she might to focus on his words to the group. She'd wondered if she'd somehow been lacking—beyond the obvious of course. Now at least she had a more logical reason for his lack of follow up.

Tanner Forsythe moved his gaze around the room studying the features of each of the men and women who now reported to him as they introduced themselves. He knew Anna would be in this group. That had been the sole reason he had stopped seeing her. But when his gaze locked in on her, when he heard her voice, he was surprised by a shock of awareness. They dated for several weeks. Once he learned that she worked for Drysdale Electronics, he had stopped seeing her immediately. Preliminary negotiations for his new position had already begun—and he did not date fellow employees. Especially when they would soon be reporting to him.

Should he have suspected she worked for Drysdale when he met her at the gym? As part of the compensation package he got membership.

He'd gone to see if he liked the facility. It was two blocks from the office, crowded after work each day. He should have pushed more at the time to find out where she worked, but he'd been more interested in Anna herself than her employer.

He was not into long-term relationships as a rule. He'd learned his lesson well from Cindy. He wasn't going to get suckered into anything like marriage again. But he and Anna had meshed in many areas. She made no demands, nor had he. They'd been two people who had a lot in common, and had ended up for one terrific night in bed.

He'd not been out with anyone else since he stopped calling her. The demands on winding up the former job and preparing for this one had been arduous. Nothing he couldn't handle, but he wanted to hit the deck running. There'd be a sizable bonus in it if he increased the bottom line within a year. Tanner was into achievement.

Forcing his attention back to the meeting, he continued to listen to the different managers and directors and wondered only briefly if Anna would cause a problem. He suspected she was too professional to make a scene in front of everybody, but with women, one never knew. He'd have to make sure their former relationship didn't throw an additional complication to the new challenge. There was enough to do to turn this business around with the competition facing it, without having to worry about any problems within.

When the last manager finished, Tanner spoke again. "I've inherited Ellie Snodgrass as my PA. She has a list of those to whom I wish to speak today. I'll keep the initial meetings short. I've been working for a number of weeks on ideas and changes in strategy, so I hope you'll show up with an enthusiasm for a new direction and a determination to see Drysdale Electronics regain the pre-eminent position in our field."

He turned to Mr. Taylor and offered his hand. "I'll do my best with your company, sir," he said.

Everyone broke into spontaneous applause at the comment.

The sound made Anna feel even worse. She felt dizzy and achy and so tired she could hardly hold up her head. Her stomach ached. She hoped she wasn't contagious. Her fellow employees wouldn't thank her if the flu ran rampant through the office.

Tanner led the way from the conference room. Everyone scrambled to their feet and quickly left except Anna. She wanted to put her head down and cry at the unexpected turn of events. Or sleep for a dozen years until she felt able to deal with things.

"Coming?" Teresa asked at the door.

Mr. Taylor's secretary Ellie peered in. She still had several packets left.

"In a minute," Anna said. Ellie came in and placed the large envelope beside Anna's notepad and left.

The silence was welcomed. Anna folded her arms on the table and rested her head on them. She had to see if her name was on today's list. If so, she prayed it was soon. Then she had the journey home—through the pouring rain, the short train ride and then the few blocks walk straight up a hill to her apartment. But once there, she could cuddle up with her cat and sleep until she felt well. Or died, whichever. It was bad enough to get the flu, but to have the shock of Tanner Forsythe as her new boss was beyond anything she'd ever anticipated.

For a moment she wished it was last August again and they had just met. First thing she'd do is tell him she worked for Drysdale.

Or maybe she should wish that they had never met at all.

She heard a sound in the hall and lifted her head. The room spun around a little, then settled. Slowly she rose, picked up her coffee cup and the thick envelope and headed for her office.

There was a note on her desk, Mr. Forsythe would see her at one o'clock.

It was only a little before ten. She had almost three hours to get through. She called Teresa's extension.

"Human Resources," her friend's secretary answered.

"This is Anna, is Teresa available?"

"No, she's in with Mr. Forsythe."

"Have her call me when she's free," Anna said. So her friend was one of the first to talk to the new man. She wondered what Teresa's assessment would be. Could Anna get her opinion about how to deal with him? She couldn't risk revealing anything. She wasn't even sure Teresa knew she'd been seeing someone, she couldn't tell her she'd slept with their new boss! She'd have to decide how to handle things on her own.

Reaching for a stack of phone messages, Anna saw several were from the East Coast. She'd get those returned first, then call the local ones. Might as well make best use of her time.

Promptly at one, Anna arrived at Ellie's desk. She'd had some soup for lunch and was feeling marginally better. The rain had tapered off. All in all, the day seemed to be improving.

"I'm here for my appointment with Mr.

Forsythe," she said. She'd brought the latest plans she and Thomas Ventner had discussed. Thomas was the current Director in Brussels. Scheduled to retire in December, he'd been grooming Anna for his position for months.

"Ben Haselton's still in there. Be another minute or two," Ellie said. "Tanner has been good about not running long with anyone." She peered at Anna. "Are you all right?"

"Think I'm coming down with the flu," Anna said. "I'm trying to stay away from everyone so I don't pass it around."

"Have a seat, dear. I take public transportation. There's no avoiding some illness during the winter months."

Anna had scarcely sat when the door opened and Ben Haselton emerged. He looked upset. Charging ahead, he didn't speak to either of them.

The buzzer sounded on Ellie's desk.

"Is Anna Larkin there?"

"She's been waiting," Ellie said, smiling at Anna.

Anna took a deep breath and rose, heading into Tanner's office like she was heading into a lion's den. She still hadn't a clue how to handle this interview. Did she pretend they had never met? Accuse him of dumping her? Or try to keep a cool facade and let him take the lead?

Tanner stood near the window that overlooked

San Francisco Bay. She entered the room and closed the door behind her. It had been shut for Ben and if anything personal was said, she'd just as soon Ellie not hear.

He turned and looked at her. For a moment their eyes met and she felt a catch in the region of her heart. He still had the ability to cause a flutter in her heart rate. She'd been well on her way for falling for the man. He'd called a halt and a good thing, too. She had her life mapped out and getting deeply involved with a man did not figure in her plans. She knew better.

"Hello, Tanner," she said, hoping he'd ask her to sit before her wobbly knees gave way.

"Anna. Have a seat. I won't keep you long. I've already spoken with Thomas in Brussels. He brought me up to speed on the European division. He said you had a few new ideas you wanted to try when you're at the helm. I'd like to see them. And get your assessment of our European standing."

So he was playing it strictly business. She could deal with that. She placed the folder on his desk. "The new plans, complete with rationale and implementation schedules, are all laid out. After you review them, I'd be happy to discuss any questions you have. Otherwise, I think you'll find Thomas's assessment matches mine—robust in the U.K. area, not so strong in Italy and France. We're running into a lot of competition from local interests. But cell phones are expanding and our new components are the best around. We just have to convince all customers of that."

He nodded, sitting behind his desk. He drew the folder over and opened it. After a minute, he looked up, studying her for a moment.

"Are you all right?"

"I will be. I think I have a touch of the flu." If she had to say that one more time today she would scream.

"Maybe you should go on home and rest up," he suggested.

"I've stuck it out this long. I can hang in the rest of the day." She wasn't going to have the new CEO think she couldn't handle her job no matter what. Or that she expected any favors. Once she might have thought she knew Tanner, but now she felt he was a stranger. The man who had shown her a fabulous time for three magical weeks was barely recognizable in the hard face opposite her.

Tanner looked back at the papers in the folder, quickly scanning them. Anna was on pins and needles watching him. Each second seemed to move in agonizing slowness. With him focused on the report, she could study him with impunity. There were new lines around his eyes, his hair was cut shorter, his business suit fit to perfection. He looked like the successful businessman he was. Had circumstances been different, she would have been immensely proud of him for achieving such a high level position at a relatively young age. He was younger than she was and already CEO of a major corporation.

She'd hesitated dating him when she'd discovered he was four years younger. She'd never been sure exactly why this dynamic thirty-four-year-old man had wanted her company. She soon forgot the age difference. They had so much in common, from liking similar kinds of movies and books, to enjoying walks along the deserted San Francisco's streets after the businesses had closed for the day. Exploring out-of-the-way streets, eating at little restaurants that were mere holes-in-the-wall had been exciting and new with Tanner.

There had been certain topics tacitly off-limits. She rarely talked about her work, nor did he talk about his. She'd been too caught up in the dizzying feelings around him, the physical attraction as well as the stimulation of their conversation. He'd been someone special.

He glanced up and caught her eye. She froze. He couldn't read minds, could he?

Closing the folder he put it to the left side of the desk where a stack of folders rested.

"I'll review this in greater detail tonight. If I have further questions, I'll call."

Taking that as a sign the interview was over, she rose swaying slightly, feeling light-headed. She gave a polite smile and turned to go. Her hand was already reaching for the knob when he spoke again. Glancing over her shoulder she saw he'd risen and was leaning casually against the side of the desk, resting on one hip.

"How are you really, Anna?" he said in that low, sexy voice of his.

She shrugged, turning slightly to better see him. "At the time I wondered why you didn't call. In light of today's events, I understand perfectly."

"If there had been any other way—" he began.

She shook her head. "We wouldn't have had that long together anyway. I'm headed for Brussels in January." She looked at him closely. "I am still headed for Brussels, right?"

He nodded. "From what Thomas Ventner and Allen Taylor have said, you are by far the best person qualified for the position. I haven't seen anything to contradict that."

She turned back to the door. Suddenly she almost doubled over in pain. Her stomach was cramping. *Please don't let me be sick in Tanner's office!*

"What the hell?" Tanner dashed around his desk to get to Anna. She clutched her abdomen, almost bent in half. The pain was sharp, but already beginning to ease. She tried breathing again. She'd be mortified if she threw up over her new boss's shoes.

"Are you in pain?" he asked the obvious.

"I need a rest room. I think I'm going to be sick again. I'm sorry!" So much for looking professional. With the way her luck was going, she'd infected him and he'd have the flu by the end of the week.

"Ellie," Tanner said, opening the door. "Can you take Anna to a rest room?"

"What's wrong?" she asked. Seeing Anna with her hand over her mouth, she swiftly put her arm around her shoulders. "We better hurry, right?"

Anna nodded.

Five minutes later Anna was splashing cool water on her face.

"You should go home," Ellie said, patting her back.

"You're right."

"Call your doctor and see if he can recommend anything to ease the symptoms."

Anna mumbled, "Nothing the doctor can do."

"Have you eaten anything today?" Ellie asked.

"I had some soup for lunch. I felt better after that. Guess I was fooling myself."

Anna hated all the fuss that was being made. All she wanted to do was slink away to her apartment, pull covers over her head and sleep the clock around. Instead she'd made a spectacle of himself in her new boss's office. Even more, she was worried Tanner would hold this against her when considering making her head of the European division.

"Still, call your doctor. It can't hurt," Ellie suggested.

Anna nodded reluctantly. "First things first, though. I'm taking a cab home. And then I'll call the doctor. But you know, the most he'll tell me is to drink plenty of fluids and get a lot of rest."

"You tried to do too much today," Ellie said. "Don't come in tomorrow unless you're feeling fit again."

"Now that's something I can easily comply with."

Within a half hour Anna was home. She gave her doctor a call, but as she suspected, he was already booked for the remainder of the day. The nurse agreed to squeeze her in early the next morning. And as Anna had predicted, the recommendation was to drink lots of fluids and get plenty of bed rest. Not a hardship. She put on her warmest nightie and made sure her cat, Mitzie, had fresh food and water then crawled into bed and pulled up the covers. In no time she was fast asleep.

The telephone woke her. It was dark. How

long had she been asleep? Anna fumbled for the phone. "Hello?"

"What did your doctor say?" Tanner asked.

CHAPTER TWO

ANNA leaned back against the pillows and groaned. She didn't want to talk to Tanner. It had been hard enough today to face him. Why was he calling? Would he do this with all employees?

"Just what I expected him to say, drink fluids and rest. What does your doctor say when you have the flu?"

"I rarely get the flu," Tanner said.

It figured, she thought.

"I'm seeing him at nine o'clock in the morning," she said. "He couldn't see me earlier. And quite frankly I wanted to be in bed and not in the waiting room the way I felt this afternoon."

"It's after nine," Tanner said. "Have you have dinner?"

She shook her head, then realized he couldn't see. Actually she didn't feel as bad as she had that morning. Maybe she was already getting better.

"I can heat a can of soup," she said.

"I'll bring a carton of soup from the deli near my place," he said.

Her eyes opened wide. "You can't come over here."

"Why not?"

"Because…because, you're now my boss."

"It's not a date, Anna, I just want to make sure you're okay. A good leader makes sure his people are in fighting shape."

"So are we fighting?" she asked, confused for a moment. She really wanted to slip back down and go back to sleep.

"No. I'm just bringing soup."

"I'll be fine. I don't want to be entertaining guests."

"You won't be entertaining me, you'll be eating the soup from the deli. You still like vegetable and beef?"

"You know it's my favorite." She cringed as soon as the words left her mouth. She was not trying to reinforce the relationship they had at one time. Anna held her breath waiting for his response.

He merely said, "I'll be there within a half hour."

Hanging up the phone, she gingerly got out of bed and went to use the bathroom. Then she brushed her hair, rinsed her mouth with mouthwash and tried to see if she looked better for having slept half the evening away.

She checked the living room to make sure it looked presentable and then continued into the kitchen to heat water for tea. Her fleece robe and fuzzy slippers kept her warm. She could hear the rain still falling outside. The thick robe was not the kind of attire she would have worn had Tanner been coming over for any other reason. That alone should clearly emphasize to him that she no longer considered them a couple. Not that he would think so. But she didn't want any wrong impressions from this visit!

Still, she checked that she had on some lipgloss before he arrived. No point in looking as bad as she felt.

When the doorbell rang a short time later, she tried to calm her nerves as she went to open the door. Raindrops glistened in his hair and on the shoulders of his jacket. Tanner carried a large bag with the deli's logo. The aroma of the hot soup immediately had her mouth watering. She took in a deep breath. Suddenly she was ravenous. She held out her hand for the bag.

"Thank you," she said.

He pushed past her and walked into the apartment as if he had every right to be there. He had visited several times when they dated so he knew his way around. Without hesitation he headed for the kitchen. Anna followed him reluctantly. She paused in the doorway and watched as he swiftly poured the hot soup into a bowl and found a spoon. She gave up and went to sit at the table.

"Eat up," he said a moment later, placing the bowl in front of her.

Anna took a taste. It was wonderful. Tanner waited until she began to eat, then rummaged around in the bag and withdrew some hot rolls. He took a plate down and put them beside her, along with a handful of wrapped butter pats.

Anna looked at him. "Did you eat?"

He nodded. Leaning his shoulder against the archway he watched her.

She became flustered. Glancing at him, she frowned. "Could you stop staring at me?"

He pushed away from the wall and came to sit beside her. Reaching out, he took one of the rolls, broke it open and buttered it.

Mitzie came in from the bedroom. She walked toward Tanner, her tail high.

"Hey, girl," he said, noticing the cat. She showed no hesitation in coming over and rubbing herself against his ankles. He leaned over and scratched her back. The loud purr indicated her delight.

"I wanted to explain about us," he said, still leaning over a little. He glanced at Anna.

She continued to eat. "It's not necessary. I figured it out today when I saw you're the new

CEO. I have my own rules against dating fellow employees. You might have mentioned the reason at the time, however." She wouldn't tell him how hurt she'd been, how confused. She'd taken weeks to get over him. For one haunting moment that morning she feared she wasn't over him. But she knew there was nothing to do but go on.

Her focus now was totally on relocating to Brussels. The brief affair they'd enjoyed was relegated to bittersweet memories. The story of her life.

"There was a lot of secrecy around the transition," he said. "Both at the company I was leaving as well as at Drysdale Electronics."

"I know how to keep my mouth closed about secrets," she said stiffly.

"It wasn't my secret to keep," he said. "But I wanted to make sure you knew that it wasn't because I didn't enjoy being with you."

Anna felt a little spurt of happiness in his words. She had wondered at the time if he had just tired of her. Or if that one night that had been so magical to her—hadn't be so special for him. She'd been totally swept away by the love they'd shared. Had he not stopped calling her, would she have convinced herself things could be different this time? Maybe she could find a man to love, who would love her.

She frowned at her wayward thoughts and concentrated on eating. The soup was delicious and so far she didn't feel queasy.

"Thank you for clearing up the situation," she said.

He laughed. "I've missed that about you, the innate politeness. What have you been up to lately?" He settled back in his chair, watching her eat. Mitzie strolled over to the sofa and leaped up, soon settled with paws beneath her.

Anna looked at him suspiciously as she reached for a roll. Taking her time to butter it slowly, she glanced at him again. "Pretty much the same as I did before I met you. I go work, I go to the gym. Occasionally I hang out with friends. I don't see you at the gym anymore."

"Once I knew you worked at Drysdale, I stopped going. I'll be starting up again now. Membership is part of my compensation package." He waited a beat, then said, "No special man?"

She almost responded but thought about it for a moment, shaking her head. "That's really not any of your business at this point is it?" she asked. It sounded better than the truth, that she hadn't even thought about seeing another man after him.

"Ouch," he said with a grimace. "No, it's not, but I'm curious."

She shrugged. "Thank you for bringing the

soup. I'm feeling much better for eating it." He'd delivered the soup, seen that she ate it. Would he leave now? She wasn't sure she wanted him to, but his staying would only lead her to regret the way things were.

"You still see the doctor tomorrow?" he asked.

"Yes, boss."

Tanner rose and leaned over Anna, resting one hand on the back of her chair and one on the table.

"Don't come into work until you're completely well. Call and tell me what the doctor says."

Feeling trapped, she glared up at him. "Don't get so close, you could get the flu."

"I'll chance it," he said and closed the short distance between them until his lips brushed hers.

Tanner left the apartment building and plunged into the rain. He strode the two blocks to where he'd left his car, annoyed with himself for reacting so strongly to seeing Anna. She looked as pale as she had that morning. He was glad he'd thought to bring her something to eat. When a person felt bad, they often didn't feel like preparing meals.

For a moment he remembered the good times they'd shared. He'd enjoyed her company more than he had anyone else in a long time. When he'd met her, it had been months since he'd been in a relationship with a woman. Jessica had been pushing for marriage, and after the disaster of his early marriage, that institution was the last thing he wanted. He'd broken it off with her last winter and concentrated on work.

Until he met Anna.

Most women followed a similar pattern—date, have fun, begin to talk about commitment and long-term. It was at that point he always cut the relationships.

But he and Anna had not reached that stage. In fact, she was the first one to ever ignore the possibility of a future together. Never once in the three or four weeks they'd dated had she even hinted. He'd been intrigued.

Now that he knew she was planning to move to Brussels at the beginning of the year it made sense.

He reached his car and climbed in, shaking some of the rain from his hair. Starting, he pulled out into traffic and headed home. He had a stack of files to review tonight, more interviews tomorrow. The thrill of the new job, the changes he planned, kept him keyed up.

Taylor had told him about each of the managers, their strengths and weaknesses. He'd been glowing about Anna. Each word emphasized

Tanner's decision not to date an employee. But he missed her. He would like to discuss company strategy, to find out more how she viewed the European market. To see if she still indulged herself with Ghiradelli chocolates and then did an extra ten minutes on the treadmill.

And, if he were honest with himself, he wanted more than a light brush of the lips.

In fact, he was surprised at how much he missed her. He hardly remembered Jessica. Before her he'd been involved with a woman named Margo. While his focus had always been on business and the push to succeed, he did like having a pretty companion to go to social events with.

With Anna it had been different. He was still attracted to her. He and Anna had laughed a lot, he remembered that. For a little while he'd thought he'd found the perfect companion—someone to relax with, to share interests and entertainment. And someone who would not expect to end up married. He should have known it was too good to last.

His rule was hard and fast. He had certain standards he adhered to and not dating a fellow employee was one—especially when she reported directly to him.

Still—she was leaving in a few weeks. Maybe they could work something out.

He shook his head, astonished he'd even give thought to such an idea. Business was business and pleasure was entirely separate. He planned to see it stayed that way!

Tonight he had a stack of files to review, tomorrow it would be back to business. Anna could take care of herself. She didn't need him bringing soup, or calling to check on her. And he certainly didn't need to be kissing her.

Anna entered the doctor's office the next morning feeling as sick as she had the day before. The brief respite she'd found last night had not lingered for long. As soon as Tanner had left, she returned to bed and slept the night away.

She refused to think about Tanner's kiss. They were no longer involved. He had made that very clear. And she had her move to Brussels to look forward to. As soon as she was well, she needed to begin getting her things packed, decide what to take and what to store at her parents' place and begin winding up her own position in the home office in preparation to her new posting in Europe.

"Miss Larkin?" One of the nurses called her from the doorway.

She showed Anna into an exam room asking her how she felt. Anna told her she was there for anything that could mitigate the symptoms of flu.

"There's not much," the nurse said as she took Anna's blood pressure. "Bed rest is about the best thing. Sometimes we can give medication that will ease the nausea and diarrhea to avoid dehydration. Do drink plenty of fluids." She noted the blood pressure reading on the chart and glanced over it. "I see it's been a while since you've been in to see the doctor."

Anna nodded. "Normally I'm as healthy as an ox." She wished she felt healthy this morning. She longed to get back to bed.

"The doctor will be only a few minutes. Why don't you change into the gown while I tell him you're here."

Normally Anna liked seeing Dr. Orsinger. He was an old-fashioned general practitioner who took a friendly interest in his patients. When he breezed into the exam room, he asked how she had been aside from the flu, jotting notes as she talked. She took that opportunity to ask him if he knew of any special medical forms she would need in anticipation of her move to Europe. He asked about the new assignment, where she would be living and for how long she would be out of the States.

He drew routine blood work, reviewed her medical history to make sure she was up-to-date on tetanus. When he finished his exam he asked her to wait a little while so that he could go online to see if there were any health alerts for Europe of which she should be aware. She agreed. Changing back into her street clothes, Anna hoped the wait wouldn't be long. She still felt shaky and tired. A short time later Dr. Orsinger returned. He looked at her oddly.

"No health crises in Europe, I hope," she said.

He motioned for her to sit down and he leaned against the edge of the counter containing the sink.

"Did you suspect you're pregnant?" he asked.

Anna stared at him, certain she had not heard correctly. He had been her doctor for years. He knew it was impossible for her to get pregnant.

"You know I cannot have children." Her voice sounded calm. She'd long ago come to terms with her inability. Except for each time when her younger sister called to announce she was pregnant. The most recent call this weekend was the third time. That hurt.

Or when her best friend had her first baby two years ago.

So most of the time she'd come to terms with her inability.

He lifted the report the nurse had given him and read it again. "Anna, we can repeat the test, but I don't think the report got mixed up."

Anna stared at him in shocked disbelief. From

the time she was sixteen years old she'd known she would never have children. The automobile accident she had been involved in had caused such great scarring both externally and internally. The external scars had faded over the years, but internally she was still messed up. Doctors had told her she would never conceive. Over the years, she'd grown used to the fact, even if she still railed against fate from time to time. She put on a good front when visiting home and seeing her sister's children or her brother's daughter. Just last weekend she had once again feigned happy recipient to the news her sister was pregnant again. Inside she'd screamed with the unfairness of life, but she let none of those feelings spill out. Even those who knew her best never had a clue how much she'd longed for a child.

It was a cruel stroke of fate that had ended that hope years ago. But she had her career.

Her career!

"I can't be pregnant." The room seemed to swirl around. She closed her eyes against the dizziness.

Tanner! Oh God. He would kill her when he found out. She had told him there was no danger of getting pregnant. He'd used a condom, it broke. She told him not to worry, she couldn't have a baby. How could this happen?

The doctor was looking at her with compassion. "Actually I believe the prognosis was it would be highly unlikely for you ever to conceive. Obviously even doctors make mistakes." He smiled at her. "I know this is a surprise, but a happy one, I hope."

"I would like a second testing please." She could not let her hopes be raised. The disappointment would be too great.

She had been in love in a college, had even been asked to marry her sweetheart—Jason Donalds. But when Jason found out she was unable to have children he'd ended their relationship so fast she hardly knew what hit her.

Since graduation, she had focused on her career to the exclusion of any long-lasting relationships. Her parents had urged her to be more open to men who were interested in her. Not every man wanted children. Adoption was an alternative if they did. But the trauma of losing Jason because she couldn't have a baby was almost too much to overcome. She was not going to risk her heart that way again.

And somehow she could not blurt out at the first introduction, "Hi, I'm Anna and I am unable to have children, you still want to date?"

The thought that she could be pregnant after all these years, after all the tests, was unfathomable. It had only been one night.

Despite the prognosis, she had always practiced safe sex the few times she'd felt close enough to a man to take the step into the bedroom. Never in a hundred years would she have suspected she could get pregnant.

Tanner was going to be furious. When she told him. Or if.

The doctor complied with her request to conduct a second set of tests. It was late morning by the time he rejoined her to confirm his original diagnosis. He spent several minutes talking with her about prenatal care, what changes she could expect in her body as pregnancy progressed and what risks were present for a woman of her age to be pregnant for the first time. With the uterus scarring, it may prove impossible to carry the child to term. He wanted to monitor her closely as the pregnancy progressed. They set up weekly appointments.

For more than half her life Anna believed she could never conceive a child. To learn she had was hard to grasp. On the way home the reality gradually seeped in. By the time she reached her apartment she was cautiously thrilled. She knew there was no guarantee, but if she'd come this far after conceiving, surely she could deliver a full-term baby.

Hurrying to the phone she quickly dialed her mother's number.

"Mom you need to sit down, I have some amazing news."

Ginny Larkin quickly raised a question about Anna's transfer.

"It's not that. I'm pregnant!" Anna blurted out.

There was silence at the other end for a long moment. Then her mother asked, "How could that be?"

"It's a miracle is how," Anna said. "I didn't believe it when the doctor told me, so I had him run the tests a second time. It's true I am pregnant. Isn't that the most amazing thing? After all these years, I'm going to have a baby!" Anna burst into tears. She felt no different from how she'd felt that morning, still feeling nausea, still tired beyond belief and a bit achy. But she didn't have the flu; she had a baby beneath her heart.

The fabulousness was beyond belief. She wanted to share the miracle with the whole world, starting with her mother. But caution took hold. She needed to wait until she was used to the fact herself and knew better if chances would improve to carry this child to term. The next few weeks would see how she progressed. The doctor had warned her to take things easy, get plenty of rest and call him if there were any signs of complications. He'd given her something for the nausea and stomach pains and urged her to eat healthy and frequently. He'd given her a prescription for prenatal vitamins. And scheduled her for an ultrasound in a month—to check the viability of the baby.

"I can't believe it," Ginny said again. "After all this time. All the doctors said it was impossible."

"The doctor is backpedaling now—saying it was highly improbable. Of course it's not impossible—I'm pregnant!" She wanted to shout it from the rooftop!

Then her mother asked, "Who's the father? I didn't know you were seeing anyone special."

Her bubble burst. Anna squeezed her eyes shut, but saw Tanner's face. She could imagine the fury when he discovered she was pregnant. Yet, there was nothing she could have done differently.

"He's a really great man, Mom. We were involved this summer. But he had a new job assignment and had to move on. We aren't seeing each other anymore." Not in the same way.

Her mother asked, "Is there any chance he'd marry you—just to give the baby a name?"

"Oh, Mom, please. I'm a competent woman. I've been on my own for years. I'll be heading up the European office of the company in a couple of months. I don't need a man to raise a baby."

"Of course you don't need one, but babies do well with both parents," her mother responded.

"Are you still going to Brussels? That's so far away. How often can I see my grandchild if he or she is five thousand miles away."

"You'll probably rack up frequent flier miles. I'll get a big enough place to have you stay over for weeks at a time."

"And your father. Your sister and brother and their families will want to see the baby. Can you take leave from work to return to have it here?"

"It's complicated, Mom. I haven't worked anything out. I just learned of the baby about an hour ago. Give me some time to get used to it and make plans."

"Well, of course. And I'm happy to help. Come home this weekend."

"I'm not sure." She wasn't feeling any better for knowing she didn't have the flu. Added to that was the stress that grew as she contemplated telling Tanner he was going to be a father. Nothing had been said in all the times she saw him about a long-term affair and especially not children.

"Tell me how you're feeling. When is it due? When will you know the sex? Have you thought of any names? I can't wait to see you. Oh, honey, I'm so delighted. I never thought— Wait until I tell your father!" Ginny's enthusiasm came across the lines like a balm to Anna's jangled nerves. She began to relax as her mother started to admonish her about eating well, sleeping extra hours and keeping up an exercise program. She urged her to take time away from work as much as possible to store up sleep—she'd need it when the baby came.

The two chatted for almost an hour. At the end of the conversation, Anna extracted a promise from her mother not to tell anyone else in the family—she wanted to share than news in a couple of weeks at the Thanksgiving holiday when everyone would be together. Reluctantly Ginny agreed.

"But how I'm going to keep this from your father, I'm not sure," she said.

"Please, Mom. This is so special. It may never happen again. I want to be there when they hear it. I want to see their expressions as well."

"I'll do it. Call me right away if you need anything."

Anna agreed and hung up. She still felt surreal. Her hand went to her stomach in the instinctive manner of all pregnant mothers.

"Hello, little one," she said softly. "I'm so glad you're here."

Tired, Anna went back to her room to lie down. She was too keyed-up to sleep, however. She began to make plans. As soon as she felt up to it, she'd visit a bookstore to get as many prenatal and newborn baby books she could locate. Then she'd have to go online and check out rentals in Brussels. The apartment Thomas Vintner had found for her wouldn't do. She needed more room.

She'd have to get baby furniture, find child care and decide what to do about school when the child was older.

And in the meantime, she had to find a way to tell the baby's daddy.

CHAPTER THREE

TANNER hung up the phone and looked at his watch. It was after two. He'd asked Ellie to check on Anna for him when she had not come into work today. She was supposed to be seen by her doctor. He wondered if she had kept the appointment. He had a few minutes before the next department head was scheduled. Unable to concentrate on the report in front of him, he dialed Anna's number. A moment later she answered.

"Did you see the doctor?" Tanner asked without preamble.

"I did," she said. "You woke me up for that? I said I would go."

"And? What was the prognosis? Could he do anything for the flu?"

"Actually he gave me some medicine for the symptoms. I'm already feeling better."

She sounded much better, he noted. Her voice had an inflection he hadn't heard for a while. He remembered their frequent talks on the phone. Before he'd go to bed many nights he'd call and they'd ramble about any and everything. He remembered each conversation, how they'd good-naturedly argue about silly things. They rarely talked seriously. Once she'd told him she had a broken engagement behind her and that she couldn't have children. That would have been the perfect opening to tell her about Zach. But the pain was still sharp when he thought of the boy, so he had kept silent.

Not that it mattered. It happened so long ago. He had to keep moving, tried to forget Cindy's betrayal and focus on the present.

Most of the time, however, their late night sessions had been lighthearted and fun. A welcome change from the stress and cutthroat business at hand. He had welcomed the diversion when negotiating this position and winding up his chief operating officer position at his prior company.

The way he calculated it, he owed Anna. More than he'd given her when he'd stopped seeing her so abruptly. They had no commitments. No long range plans. But it still had to have hurt when he stopped seeing her with no word. He could have said business was too intense and he had to call a halt. It would have been better than silence.

"That's good." *I was worried about you* sounded too personal. Yet he had been. He'd never seen her look so frail as she had on Monday.

"Thank you for your concern. I'll probably take the rest of the week off and be back on Monday," she said. "I have lots of sick leave on the books. I'm never sick."

"Get better. Call if you need anything." He knew she had an exemplary attendance record as well as outstanding performance reviews. She hadn't risen as high as she had in the company without a strong work ethic.

He replaced the receiver on his phone and looked at the stack of papers on his desk. He had made the right decision to sever their relationship. But for a moment, he enjoyed hearing her voice.

It had been a pleasure dating Anna. He missed the easy way they could talk about everything, or remain silent for long stretches without any awkwardness. He liked the fact she enjoyed similar activities. The way she jumped on and off the cable car like a native. Her love of crab cocktails at the Wharf. Her delight in watching kites flying at the marina.

He rose and paced to his window. Glancing out on Montgomery Street, he remembered the Sunday afternoon they'd walked along the deserted thoroughfare peeking into some of the windows of the closed shops and businesses. They had made up stories about who owned them, the kind of businesses they were and the dreams of the future the owners were likely to have. Then thcy had hiked to the wharf to have crab cocktails and sourdough bread for lunch. That had been two days prior to the discovery that she worked for Drysdale Electronics. His own code of ethics had demanded he stop seeing her. For once he wished he wasn't so good about following his own rules.

He walked to his office door and opened it. Ellie was working diligently on her computer.

"Order some flowers for Anna Larkin," he said. "Have them delivered today."

Ellie looked up in surprise. "Sure thing. Is she worse?"

"No, but she is going to stay home a few days to get over the flu."

"What shall I put on the card?" Ellie asked.

"Best wishes from your friends at Drysdale Electronics," Tanner said. He didn't want to give rise to speculation with the rest of the staff. But he wanted some flowers to brighten her apartment.

He returned to his desk better able to focus on the work. But always in the back of his mind was the image of Anna he had seen last night in her warm pink fleece robe and fluffy slippers. He felt a tightening in his stomach any time he thought about her. Why wasn't she as easy to forget as other women he had dated over the years? Was it only because they were forced into proximity from now on? Or was there something particularly special about Anna Larkin? He could almost feel her soft skin under his fingertips. Smell her special scent. Hear her laughter and see the sparkle in her eyes.

He'd need a cold shower if he didn't stop daydreaming about her. Turning, he plunged back into work finding relief in the myriad of facts to be absorbed.

Anna spent the next few days lounging around her apartment, sleeping as much as she could. She had been delighted with the bouquet of flowers from the office the day she'd learned her news. She took them as a positive omen. A celebration—though only she knew why. The lavish arrangement of colorful fall flowers with chrysanthemums and other blossoms raised her spirits whenever she looked at it.

When not resting, she went on the Internet to search sites about pregnancy and newborns. She studied housing listings for Brussels. She had so much to think about. First to make it through the pregnancy. She'd follow the doctor's orders to the letter. Any risk would be ruthlessly dealt with. She yearned for this baby with all in her.

She needed to find a flat in Brussels larger than originally planned. She'd have to furnish a room for a child. Perhaps she could hire a live-in nanny or au pair to help out with the baby once he or she was born. That would require an even larger place—especially if she wanted room for her family to stay.

Would it be a boy or girl? She had no preference. Daydreaming about either, she let her imagination soar. A tough little boy like Tanner, charging ahead, learning things fast, making a difference. Breaking hearts.

Or a little girl. Would she have dark hair like her daddy? Sparkling eyes full of mischief?

Either would be loved to bits. She prayed it would be healthy—and that she could deliver her baby safely into the world.

She also had to decide when to tell people. Because of the high risk of miscarriage throughout the pregnancy she didn't want to tell anybody until the doctor gave her some encouragement things would work out.

How cruel to be granted this precious wish and have it snatched away if she miscarried. Once again she searched the Internet for high-risk pregnancies and ways to get around the problems. There was no getting around the scarring; the rest she'd do her best to minimize.

She would tell her family in a couple of weeks at Thanksgiving. They would rejoice with her news. And be there if the unspeakable happened.

She knew the exact day they had made love—it wasn't everybody who could say exactly when a child was conceived. She was not quite two months along but after Christmas the first trimester would have passed. If she were still pregnant, and had her doctor's blessing, she'd tell friends then. She wanted everyone to know before she moved to Brussels. It was so much better to hear it in person rather than via e-mail or a letter.

Though she still had the problem of how to tell Tanner. And when. She could imagine his reaction—she suspected he would not be happy. The last thing he wanted was to get tangled up with anybody. Dating was fine—even having a steady relationship for a few weeks fit his game plan. She'd have to make sure he knew she expected nothing from him. Should she wait to tell until right before she left for Europe? Or maybe waiting until she was in Brussels would be safer.

Safer? What did she expect, he'd change his mind about her transfer?

Actually she hadn't a clue how he'd take the news—but she didn't feel it would be a warm and happy reaction.

She dreaded the confrontation. Brainstorming different ways to relay the news, she didn't have a comfortable plan by end of the day. Maybe something would come to her soon.

By Saturday, Anna was going crazy being cooped up. The rain had passed and the day was glorious. The mild medication the doctor had prescribed had cleared up her nausea and the endless hours of rest had her feeling fit again.

She bundled up against the breeze coming off the Bay and headed for the marina. There was a large bookstore there that would have everything she needed.

As she walked along, her spirits soared. It was a beautiful day and she was pregnant! She couldn't wait until she showed and the entire world would know with just one glance.

Spending hours browsing in the bookstore, Anna finally emerged with six books, one on what to expect during pregnancy and five on child care. She had watched her sister's children from time to time, and always rocked the babies when they were little, but this was different. She would be responsible for the entire care of this child. She needed to learn so much. She wanted to be the best mother possible.

She was only a couple of blocks from the wharf. Since it was so pretty, and she was loathe to return to her apartment this soon, she decided to walk to Pier 39 and have something to eat. Frequent small meals were the key to ending the nausea according to her doctor.

One of the treats at the Pier was the bunch of sea lions at the end. Their antics always caused laughter. She could hear their hoarse barking from blocks away. Feeling buoyed by the day, she almost walked on air. When the baby was older and they visited the States, she'd bring him or her to see the sea lions. There was so much she wanted to share with her child.

Her favorite city spot on the Bay was as crowded as most Saturdays. She dodged in-line skaters, kite fliers and families with children running back and forth. The tourists lined up to ride the excursion boats. Joggers ran along the outside of the wide sidewalks, dodging the occasional pedestrian that veered into their paths. The breeze was brisk, cool and refreshing. She shifted the bag of books to her other hand and looked around with interest. She loved people watching.

"Anna?"

She recognized that voice. Stunned, she looked

over her shoulder. Tanner veered from the edge of the sidewalk to jog over to her. He'd obviously been running a while. His long legs showed beneath dark blue shorts. His T-shirt was marked with perspiration. His hair was totally wind-blown. Gone was the staid business professional. He looked hot and sexy. Her eyes drank in every inch. He looked like he had at the gym, fit and athletic, and gorgeous enough to stop her heart.

"Hi," she said. They'd never gone jogging together, but they had discussed it a couple of times. Golden Gate Park had wonderful jogging trails through the eucalyptus groves and on out to the ocean. She'd thought they'd explore some of them together. But that was before he stopped calling.

"Feeling better, I take it. You look good," he said.

She nodded, pleased with the compliment. "First day out. I couldn't stand to stay in the apartment a minute longer. I see you're getting some exercise."

"First time this week. It's been hectic, as I'm sure you'd expect. Long hours, lots to review even when I get back to the apartment at night."

"Talked to everyone?"

"All the managers. I'm getting some resistance in certain quarters. Nothing I can't handle," he said confidently.

She could imagine Tanner handling anything.

Except—maybe her announcement. Of course she instantly wanted to tell him. Yet she wasn't ready. And if the baby didn't make it, there'd be no reason to tell him. She wasn't sure which way to go.

"Want to grab a cup of coffee?" he asked. "That is if you don't mind being seen with me like this."

Anna hesitated. His attire was the least of it. She was suddenly conscious of the books in the bag, of the secret she kept. Yet a part of her yearned to spend a few more minutes in his company. She had missed him over the last few weeks. Soon she'd be living thousands of miles away and any chance of running into him would vanish.

"I might be talked into a fruit smoothie," she said. There were several places on the Pier that offered caffeine-free beverages.

He fell into step as they headed toward the Pier. "Been shopping?"

"Just a few books to while away the time. I wish I'd had them this week." She hoped he wouldn't ask her titles. They shared a liking of mysteries. Quickly to forestall him, she asked, "Did you finish your run? Or am I interrupting?"

"I was winding down," he said. "You're not interrupting."

"So how was your first week?" She had mixed emotions, knowing she would not be at the head office long to watch Tanner in action. She was excited about her promotion, however, and couldn't wait to head an entire division herself. Maybe he'd give her some pointers about taking over from someone who was retiring.

"Exhilarating," he said. "There is so much more challenge at Drysdale than I had my previous place. That was a growing company and had its own set of challenges. With Drysdale Electronics I have to reverse some ill advised decisions to regain market share. The company is larger and more diverse, so the challenges greater."

She laughed. "And you thrive on challenges. I bet some old-timers believe we're doing just fine. My guess is Bill White was a pain in the butt and Marcie Longstreet had more ideas than you could ever implement—even if any of them would be profitable."

"You do know the people who work there," he said.

A youngster ran full tilt into Anna, looking at the balloon floating above him rather than where he was going. Tanner put his arm around her shoulders to steady her.

"Watch where you're going or you'll lose that balloon," he told the child.

The little boy looked scared for a minute, then muttered an apology and ran around them.

"Where are his parents?" Anna asked, trying to ignore the rush of excitement Tanner's touch brought. She could feel him through her sweater. For one moment she wished she could lean against him and claim some of his strength. But she stepped away and looked around to see who was responsible for the child. She would never let her child be unattended in such a crowded place. Danger lurked everywhere. For a moment the thought of guarding her child's safety seemed daunting. How did parents manage?

"I don't know, but I'm sure they are nearby. They better watch him—he could get lost quickly in this crowd."

Her shoulders had been warm from his touch. Now she felt the cool breeze from the Bay. She tried to quell her rapid heart rate. For a moment, she'd felt a shock of awareness. Had he felt anything? If so, he gave nothing away. He'd touched her frequently when they dated. She'd loved the feeling. It was hard to remember to keep her distance now.

When they reached the long pier converted from servicing cruise ships to supporting dozens of shops that catered to tourists. They walked partway down the wooden structure and soon found an available outdoor table. Tanner ordered their drinks while Anna sat in the sunshine. The sun kept the temperatures manageable, though she wondered if Tanner would get cold in his skimpy attire now that he was no longer running.

"Strawberry smoothie," he said, setting the drink down for her.

He sat opposite her with a large hot coffee.

"Ready to return to work Monday?" he asked.

"Yes. I kept in contact with my secretary, but it's not the same as being there to keep on top of things. I probably could have come in yesterday, but indulged myself with an extra day. I've slept more this week than I think I have in years. So now I'm rested, and raring to go."

She was getting used to the idea of the baby, but since it wouldn't be born before June, she wanted to get back to work—to fill her days so she didn't constantly dwell on the coming changes. Or the possibility of loss.

"No one else has come down with the flu," he commented. "So I guess you weren't contagious."

She took a sip of her beverage feeling guilty. She'd thought she had the flu at the time, but had not corrected that assumption. "Good." He had better hope she wasn't contagious or he'd have a bunch of women out on maternity leave at the same time.

She needed to consider her own leave of absence. Should she fly home to have the baby in

California as her mother suggested? Or have her mother fly to Brussels while Anna remained there? Another decision to make. She could see advantages to both scenarios.

Tanner studied her for a moment.

"What?" she asked, feeling uncomfortable. His dark eyes were compelling. She remembered gazing into them when they were making love. Her pulse pounded. She sipped her drink again, trying to break the spell.

"I'm curious about your transfer to Brussels," he said. "You've been at head office since you started. Why move so far away? Your family's in California, you must have lots of friends here."

"Yes to both. But this is something I've wanted for years. I've studied French in anticipation of this opportunity. Every vacation lately has been to Europe, several weeks spent in the Brussel's office—learning all I can about the people I'll be dealing with and the ways of doing business. It's going to be a huge challenge. But one that I can handle." Great, she sounded like she was interviewing for the position. Mr. Taylor had told her it was a done deal.

Yet things could change. She best not forget she was talking to the new CEO of the company, who had the power to grant or deny this move.

"From what I've learned this week, you're a

good choice. Thomas speaks highly of your ideas. I liked the report you gave me. It shows a depth that surprised me from someone dealing with things from San Francisco instead of on site."

She nodded, delighted in his comments.

"I'll miss you," Tanner said unexpectedly.

She looked at him in surprise. "I'll call every so often," she said. "And keep you fully apprised."

"You, Anna. Not the director. I enjoyed our dates."

"I did, too. But we both know you were wise to call a halt. How awkward if would be if we were still seeing each other."

She still remembered how his muscles felt beneath her fingertips. Not the memories she should have of her CEO. She could almost feel the exquisite pleasure his mouth had brought. She looked away before she made an idiot of herself. It might prove awkward, but she missed him. She'd drawn closer to Tanner in the short weeks they'd dated than any other man since Jason.

"I need to get going. Thanks for the drink." She picked up the cup to take with her and reached for the book bag. It snagged on the corner of the bench and scattered the contents on the ground.

Tanner rose quickly and reached down to pick them up. He paused as he read the titles.

Anna froze. She couldn't move. Each word

seemed to jump off the covers. Could she bluff her way through? Say the books were for a friend?

He looked at her, his expression ferocious. "What the hell is this?"

CHAPTER FOUR

"Books for a friend?" she tried, staring at the damning titles, not meeting his eyes. She had to look as guilty as sin.

"Books bought to while away the hours, you said. Nothing about being for a friend. These are books about babies and— Oh, God, are you pregnant?"

She reached for the books, tugging them from his resisting fingers. Stuffing them back in the bag, she scooped up her drink and turned. His hand wrapped around her arm, holding her in place.

"Answer my question." His voice sounded like a low growl.

"If I am is it any business of yours?" She tried bravado. She would not be intimidated!

"Dammit to hell, yes, if the baby's mine. And you weren't seeing anyone but me recently. There was no flu, you have morning sickness."

"I thought I had the flu."

"You told me you could *not* get pregnant. What

are you trying to pull? Force a marriage? It won't work, babe, I'm not getting caught in that trap again. If that's your plan, forget it."

She yanked her arm free. "I'm not trying anything." She hurried away. But he followed close beside her.

"Answer my question," he said again.

"Yes, I am pregnant," she bit out, increasing her pace. He easily kept up with her.

"You said—"

She stopped and swung around to face him. "Let's get one thing clear, Tanner. I was in a bad car crash when I was sixteen. I went through the windshield. There was glass everywhere. Due to the scarring, I was told I would never conceive, never have a baby. My fiancé dropped me like a hot potato when he learned of that. For more than twenty years I've believed I would never have a child, never be a mother. I can't explain what happened and neither can my doctor. I'm not exactly risk free with this pregnancy, but to me it's a miracle of monumental proportions. So I'm sorry if it upsets you, I'm thrilled to death!" She ended up almost yelling at him.

"Now stay away from me! I don't want anything more to do with you!" She turned and headed for the street. Surely she could find a cab and get home before she burst. She was furious.

How dare he think she'd try to trap him into marriage. Get real—what century was he living in? Her anger grew that he suspected she had some angle to play. Hadn't he gotten to know her at all when they'd been seeing each other? What she'd told him was true, this was a huge miracle and she would give thanks for her child every day of her life—if she was able to deliver a healthy baby. Her doctor had not been at all certain about that possibility.

Let Tanner go his own way. Neither she nor the baby needed him.

Tanner spun around, wishing there was something he could put his fist through! Uttering an expletive, he clenched his hands. The sudden anger threatened to explode! He turned back and watched Anna get into a cab. Dammit it to hell! He did not need this. He'd thought Anna someone he could trust. He'd even been trying to rationalize their seeing each other from time to time—like the times he needed an escort to some formal event. Or even have them get together for coffee on the weekend and discuss the company business.

He'd been played for a fool like before—with Cindy.

The first time could be excused. Especially since he'd been a twenty-one-year-old kid at the time. But he'd been around the block more than once since then. How could he have trusted her? They should have taken steps when they discovered the condom had been faulty. *He* should have taken steps.

God, he was going to be a father. He'd avoided any serious entanglement with a woman since his divorce—to protect his heart. He wasn't sure he could go through something like this again. Not if he lost the baby like he lost Zach. He clenched his teeth against the old familiar ache. He kept his anger white-hot against Cindy, but it never changed a thing.

Tanner didn't know how long he stood on the busy sidewalk after Anna left. Finally he realized he was growing cold. The day was not one for standing around in shorts. He began running again. He headed for home, and the decisions that had to be made.

Once at his apartment, he quickly went to change. He stood beneath the shower for a long time, until the water ran cold. He couldn't believe it. For a moment the sheer magnitude of the situation was overwhelming. A child. A baby. A boy or girl he didn't plan on. What was he going to do? How dare Anna dismiss his legitimate concerns when the condom broke and delay any action until too late! He was furious.

And awed.

A child of his own.

What would he do with an infant?

What did Anna expect of him? She had not told him—he'd had to find out accidentally.

Would she ever have told him? The thought brought another flare of anger. Was she planning to move to Brussels and never even *tell him?*

How dare she try such a trick. She'd soon learn he hadn't gotten where he was in the business world by being nice. She'd begin by making demands. This time, he knew how to counter. There would be no repeat of the past.

He toweled off and donned dark slacks and a pullover top. Hesitating only a moment, he went to the bedroom closet and reached up into the back corner, taking down the small box. Tanner sat on the edge of the bed and removed the lid. A handful of photographs and a few papers were all that were in the box.

He lifted the pictures. The top one was of Cindy in the hospital with Zach. He was so tiny. The nurses had bundled him tightly in the blanket, only his little face and fat cheeks showed. He put it to the back of the pile and looked at the next one. Him holding Zach. For a moment Tanner could feel the light weight of the infant, smell the baby scent of powder and milk. The next picture showed a chubby baby lying on a bed, kicking his feet in the air. Tanner felt a clutch in his heart.

Slowly he reviewed the photos, staring for a long moment at the last one, showing the little boy standing. He'd taken his first steps right before this picture. Zach had been just over a year.

There were no more pictures.

Tanner took a deep breath, feeling again the loss of the son he'd only known for a year. He gathered the pictures and put them back in the box. In only a moment, he'd returned the container to the closet and headed for his office.

Hunting for the number, he lifted the phone and called Anna.

Anna had prepared herself a cup of herbal tea and taken the first book to the sofa. She was reclining with the book in hand when the phone rang.

"What do you mean not risk-free?" Tanner asked.

She gripped the receiver tightly. "It means the scarring had not miraculously disappeared, it still poses problems as the fetus develops. I could spontaneously miscarry at any time. There could be other complications. I'm not exactly a young woman—not to be having a first baby."

"So you may not deliver?" he asked gently.

"Exactly. On the other hand, my doctor is going to watch me carefully and do all he can to make sure I do have a healthy baby. And I was planning to tell you, I just hadn't decided when, or how. I only found out myself on Tuesday."

"You could have called me," he said.

She could hear the control he held on his voice. She knew he was angry. But she was angry at him for his comments at the Pier.

"I'm not telling most people yet. The doctor said he'd have a better feeling for how it would go as time goes by."

"I'm not most people."

She took a breath. He was right, but still—she wanted to handle things her way.

There was a moment of silence, then Tanner said, "How are you feeling?"

"Lousy. I have morning sickness, I feel achy and I have some discomfort in the abdomen area probably because of the internal scarring and the growing baby. But I have some medication for the nausea and am nibbling something every couple of hours, so I should be fit for work on Monday."

"So you really didn't believe you could have a baby."

"I truly did not," she said solemnly. "I was not trying to trap you into anything—let alone marriage. For heaven's sake, Tanner, I'm going to Brussels in a few weeks. You live here. What kind of relationship would that be?"

For a second she imagined they were still involved. Would they have moved to a closeness she had only felt with Jason? Or would the demands of work have proved too much and they would have drifted away.

"When do you see the doctor again?"

"Next Tuesday. And every Tuesday after that."

"Keep me informed," he said.

"If anything changes."

"I want to know everything about the pregnancy."

Anna bristled slightly. She didn't like his tone, yet she couldn't help feel slightly mollified that he was concerned for the baby. And her own health?

"I'll keep you apprised." It would be like a work project. Weekly updates. "Goodbye, Tanner."

Anna hung up the phone and drew the baby book near again. She had so much to learn.

Monday morning Anna arrived at work early. She had spent the remainder of the weekend worrying about Tanner and his initial reaction. Somehow she had to make him see that she was not looking to force them into any kind of arrangement that had long-range implications. He had not called again, so maybe he had thought things over and calmed down.

There was plenty of work to do, as the stacks of papers on her desk attested. She had, after all, been gone for several days. She plunged right into it—starting with a phone call to Thomas in Brussels before he left for home.

By two o'clock she had read all of her mail and scanned the telephone messages—returning the most urgent and delegating several to people who reported to her.

Her secretary had popped in when she first arrived bringing her up-to-date on what had happened in the company over the last few days. Apparently Tanner was wasting no time in cutting waste, rearranging personnel and generally making changes that had everyone nervous and wary. Two of the senior managers had been let go. There had been some shuffling among the other employees in various departments, and another management meeting had been called for tomorrow morning.

So far he'd left her division alone. She hoped it continued that way. She could defend her staff and her projects.

Still, she worked diligently, wanting nothing to give rise for Tanner to question her abilities. She never forgot he had the final veto power for her promotion and transfer to Europe.

Anna took a quick walk at lunch. The weather remained sunny and cold with a brisk breeze blowing in from the Bay. She was more conscious than ever of taking good care of herself. Fresh air and exercise would become her new watchword.

As she strolled down Montgomery Street, she remembered the Sunday afternoon she and Tanner had walked along these same sidewalks. They'd been practically deserted, not bustling with people as today.

She missed the fun they'd shared. Missed meeting him on the spur-of-the-moment for coffee or a meal. Missed the late night calls. Loneliness was not a stranger, but for a few weeks, Tanner had kept it at bay.

Despite her own efforts to remain aloof, she'd enjoyed being part of a couple for those weeks.

The most astonishing thought struck. She could get married. She no longer was a woman who could not give her husband a baby. Jason's reasons for leaving had hurt for many years. Her pregnancy blew them away. Granted, she wouldn't be completely certain of anything until she held her baby in her arms, but the possibilities multiplied.

Maybe she could find a man to love, who would love her. She'd enjoyed being part of a couple. Having a family life like her parents and siblings enjoyed. Be normal.

Tanner had given her a gift beyond price. She was free to be a normal woman again for the first time since Jason had broken her heart when he left. Of course her initial thought was of Tanner Forsythe. She quickly squelched even the hint of dreams in that direction. His reaction at the marina on Saturday had made a definite impression.

Shortly after lunch, she received a phone call from Ronald Franklin, who introduced himself as Tanner's attorney.

"My client is concerned about the information he learned this weekend," the attorney began.

"I thought I made it clear to your client that there was nothing to worry about," she said with some asperity. It sure hadn't taken Tanner long to raise defenses. Hadn't he listened to her when she said she wanted nothing from him?

"Do you deny that he is the father of the baby?" Ronald asked.

"I do not," she replied. "However I am not asking for anything from him."

"We would require DNA testing."

"Why? I'm not asking for anything so does it matter?" Wasn't this man listening, either?

"It's highly unlikely that you would reject the financial benefits, if nothing else, of having

Tanner as the father of your child. My client is a wealthy man."

"I don't need his money. I don't need his interference. And I won't even be in the country after January."

"Where are you going?" he asked. She heard the ruffling of papers in the background. Was he searching for that fact?

"I've been transferred to Europe and will be working in our office in Brussels. I have no immediate plans to return to the United States once I'm there, so you can assure your client that he has nothing to worry about. Now, if you'll excuse me, I have work to do."

Anna hung up calmly, really wanting to slam down the receiver. How dare Tanner get an attorney involved! She had made no demands of him. She debated storming into his office to confront him, but knew that would do nothing but cause speculation and rumors to arise. Thus far the two of them had kept their relationship quiet and she'd just as soon see it continued that way.

By four-thirty Anna was tired. She gathered her things and told her secretary she was leaving for the day.

"Still feeling a bit wonky after the flu?" Peggy asked.

Anna almost confided the situation to her, but she did not want to make it known until the first trimester was safely passed. "Just too much work after so many days off. You feeling okay?"

"I'm fine," Peggy said with a wave.

Anna started toward the underground station, then changed her mind. Hailing a cab, she settled back to enjoy the ride home. Taking public transit made her more susceptible to any germs floating around. She needed to rethink her normal mode of transportation in the future and rely on taxis until she moved to Europe.

The next day Anna received another call from Ronald Franklin suggesting that his client and she meet to discuss the situation.

"I cannot make it any clearer," she said. "I am making no demands on Tanner Forsythe. I don't see the need to get together to discuss anything."

However, as soon as she hung up from talking to him, she called her friend Stephanie. Stephanie worked in a large attorneys group. Anna had never had need of an attorney before. She wanted her friend's help to steer her into the right direction.

"Hey, what's up?" Stephanie said when she recognized Anna's voice.

"A small legal complication has arisen. I don't want to go into details now. I'll fill you in on everything as soon as I can. I need a good attorney."

"Criminal case?" Stephanie asked, her manner at once professional.

"No, civil, I think." Or was it called family law? She wasn't sure.

"I need a little more info so I'll know which attorney to recommend," Stephanie said.

Anna checked to make sure her door was still shut tightly then lowered her voice.

"It's about a parental issue for an unborn child."

"Whose?" Stephanie asked.

"Mine."

There was stunned silence on the other end. Then Stephanie responded in a very professional tone. "Jillian Stevens is our best attorney for Family Court. Shall I transfer your call to her now or give you her number so you can call at your convenience?"

Anna smiled. Her friend must have a million questions, yet kept her professionalism.

"Transfer me, please. And I promise, Steph, that as soon as I can, I'll give you all the lowdown."

Anna quickly made an appointment to visit Jillian Stevens that very afternoon. With the doctor's appointment and now one for the attorney, she wasn't going to get much work done today.

As soon as she'd hung up the phone, her secretary popped in and said she was wanted in the

CEO's office. Glancing at the clock Anna saw it was too early for the managers meeting. So was this a personal confrontation or strictly business? She gathered the folder of the most recent activities and walked calmly to Tanner's office. Her heart beat double-time. She was nervous and wary. Ready to stand up for herself if the need arose, but hoping it was business. She didn't want to dwell on the personal.

Ellie smiled warmly when she arrived.

"You look much better. Glad you're back. The good news is nobody else seems to have come down with the flu, so you must not have been contagious."

Anna smiled. It would be a miracle if what she had had been contagious.

"Mr. Forsythe wanted to see me," she said.

"Call him Tanner," Ellie said. "He's asked everybody to do so. Let me tell him you're here." She spoke into the phone and a moment later nodded to her to go right in.

Taking a deep breath Anna pushed the door open and stepped into Tanner's office. He sat behind his large desk. The tall glass window behind him gave a wide view of the city and a glimpse of the bay. He looked up when she walked in but didn't speak for a moment.

Anna took the plunge. "I brought the latest projections from my department," she said. "I've been in touch with Tom who gave me some more recent figures. You wanted them last week, but since I wasn't here, I hope today is soon enough."

He held out his hand for the folder and motioned her to take a seat. Scanning the top page quickly, he tossed it on the desk and looked at her.

"I heard from Ronald that you are not willing to meet to discuss the situation," he said.

"That's right. There's nothing to discuss."

"I am not the naïve young man I once was. This time things will be done my way."

"What do you mean?" she asked. This time?

"I mean I will take steps to ensure my rights," Tanner said.

"I'm seeing an attorney myself this afternoon. I'm asking her to draw up papers releasing you from all parental responsibilities. I'm not trying to trap you into marriage or demand child support or anything."

"It's my child, too," he said. "Maybe I want certain rights."

"Make up your mind. Saturday you accused me of coming after you for some sort of scam, the next minute when you hear I do not need any help, you're indignant that I'm trying to keep him from you."

"Him?"

"Or her. It's too early to determine the sex of

the child at this point. I'm sure my attorney can be in touch with yours to alleviate any concerns you have as to my motives. That should satisfy you."

Tanner threw his pencil onto the desk and leaned back in the chair studying Anna.

"I would be interested in hearing your proposition."

"No proposition, simply a release for you to sign relinquishing parental responsibilities."

"Even if I would agree to such a thing, how do you propose to raise this child?"

Anna looked at him warily. "What do you mean? I make a good salary. I have investments and savings. I'll be able to find child care in Brussels as easily as I find it here in San Francisco. This child will be well loved and cared for. My mother is already over the moon knowing there may be a baby. My family will be delighted for me. No one ever thought—" She stopped abruptly. Tanner wasn't interested.

"That there would be a baby?" he asked quickly.

"I wasn't lying when I told you I could not get pregnant. I have been told that since the accident when I was a teenager. I plan to tell my family at Thanksgiving, if I'm still pregnant then."

He studied her for a moment, then said, "What

about my parents? They will also be the child's grandparents."

Anna hadn't considered that aspect. Was she doing a disservice to her child to deny him or her interaction with its father? With relatives from Tanner's side of the family?

She got along well with all her grandparents, especially her grandma Sarah, her father's mother. And her aunts and Uncle Clell. How would she have felt growing up to only know her mother's side of the family?

"That will have to be worked out," she said. She hoped talking with the attorney later in the day would settle things. However, there was more to consider than she initially thought.

"This is my baby, too," Tanner said softly.

Anna nodded, remembering the night this precious gift had been conceived. She had not dated for several months prior to meeting Tanner. And she had not been out on a single date since they stopped seeing each other. All her adult life she believed business would always be her primary focus. Now it seemed as if she had another option.

She delighted in the knowledge that there was the possibility in the few months to hold her child in her arms. She would do almost anything to assure that happened. Even if she had to take a leave of absence from work to keep the pregnancy viable.

She rose. "I will have my attorney call yours after I've talked with her." She turned and left the office, ignoring Tanner's voice calling her to stay.

Anna was the first one out of the meeting later; she was not taking the chance of getting cornered by Tanner before she talked to the attorney. She had so much to consider.

Jillian Stevens was an older, no-nonsense woman who cut right to the chase. She asked the circumstances about the pregnancy and then quickly proposed several scenarios on how Anna could handle the situation. From shared custody, to sole custody, to relinquishing of parental rights of the father, to even giving up the baby for adoption.

Anna quickly told her that she planned to keep the child and explained how miraculous the conception had been.

"So the father is out of it?" Jillian asked, jotting notes on a yellow tablet.

"We had stopped seeing each other several weeks before I found out I was pregnant. When he learned of the pregnancy, his initial reaction was to accuse me of trying to trap him into marriage. In fact, he's had his attorney call me to discuss the legal aspects. That's why I came to see you."

"And what do you expect me to do?" Jillian asked.

"I thought a complete relinquishing of parental rights would reassure him that I have no designs on him. You could draw up such a form, right?"

"And what about the rest of his family? Are there grandparents, aunts and uncles? Do you not plan to let your baby know any of his biological family on his father's side?"

Anna bit her bottom lip. "I really never considered all of that," she said. "My mother is thrilled with the news. The rest of my family will be delighted once I tell them. I want my baby to know its family. I just don't know how to manage that with Tanner's side."

"I suggest that you and Tanner sit down together and talk about all the ramifications and alternatives that are available," Jillian said. "I'm happy to draft up whatever agreement you come to, but you two need to decide what that agreement is. I'm going to give you a packet of materials that gives an overview of the various options I outlined. I hope it will answer all the questions and concerns you have, including some you may not have thought of. After you've had time to review the information, I strongly urge you to discuss the situation with Tanner Forsythe. For the sake of your baby if nothing else, I hope you can keep it cordial."

Anna was tired by the time she reached home. Things were getting more complicated every day. After the attorney's visit, she'd seen the doctor. At least things were stable on that front. She opened the door to the surprising aroma of spaghetti sauce.

"Hello?" she called, turning to close the door.

"Anna, darling," her mother came bustling out of the kitchen.

"Mom?" Anna couldn't believe her eyes. She hadn't expected to see her mother. They'd spoken on the phone again over the weekend and she'd said nothing about driving over to visit. Anna flung the packet of papers and her purse on the sofa and ran to hug her mother.

CHAPTER FIVE

"I COULDN'T stay away," Ginny Larkin said. "I am so thrilled about the news. Your father is, too. And he's having a hard time keeping it quiet. I had to tell him, but he's not telling your sister or brother." Holding her daughter at arm's length, Ginny studied her for a minute. "You don't look so well," she said.

Anna laughed. "Gee thanks, Mom, that makes me feel really good. Truth is I am so tired I can hardly see straight. As I told you, I took off time last week and slept round the clock. I thought I was ready to return to work, but now I just want to sleep again for a week."

"I remember that feeling well. I had three pregnancies to get through. This is just your first."

Anna hadn't thought about it that way. If she could get pregnant once, she could get pregnant again. How lucky could one woman get?

Her mother looked closely. "You are okay, right?"

"I saw the doctor again today and he said I'm doing fine. I'm not sick every moment, just tired."

"So go change into something more comfortable and lay down for a little while. I'll call you when dinner's ready."

Anna didn't need to be told twice. She headed for the bedroom already unbuttoning her blouse and ready to shed all of her business attire. She put on her long flannel nightgown, and over that she threw on her chenille robe. Crawling onto the bed she planned to just close her eyes for a few minutes. Mitzie jumped up beside her, stretching out along Anna's side. She relished the cat's warmth.

Laying back against the pillows she relaxed and felt her body give way into sleep.

It seemed like only seconds later the doorbell sounded. The noise jarred Anna awake. Mitzie jumped off and headed regally toward the living room. Anna sighed, then threw back the afghan, slipped her feet into warm fuzzy slippers and headed for the living room. Glancing back at the clock near her bed, she realized she'd been asleep almost half an hour. She heard her mother answer the door a moment later.

"May I help you?" Ginny asked.

By then Anna was far enough into the living room to see Tanner standing in the doorway. He looked startled to see her mother.

"Is Anna here?" he asked.

"Yes, I'm here," Anna said before her mother could reply. "Mom, This is Tanner Forsythe," Anna said, self-conscious of her attire. Tanner would think this was all she wore when home.

"He's the new CEO at Drysdale. My new boss. Come in, Tanner. What can I do for you?" she asked. Why was he here? She glanced at her mother, wondering if she'd pick up on anything. She did not want her mother getting involved at this stage.

Tanner stepped inside and raised an eyebrow as he took in Anna's attire. "I didn't mean to get you out of bed," he said. "I thought you were feeling better."

Anna shrugged. "I was just resting before dinner. Have a seat."

"Dinner will be ready in ten minutes, Anna. Would you like to invite Mr. Forsythe to join us?" her mother asked.

No! The last thing Anna wanted was Tanner and her mother becoming chummy. Yet her mother had instilled polite behavior in all her children. She couldn't very well refuse without raising more questions than she wanted to deal with.

But before she could figure out how to refuse without giving her mother ideas, Tanner smiled at Ginny. "That would be delightful, however, I have made other plans."

Anna's mother smiled warmly. "Another time, perhaps."

Anna waited until her mother returned to the kitchen before she sat on a chair near the sofa and looked warily at Tanner. "What do you want?" she asked quietly, keeping an eye on the kitchen door.

"We need to talk," he said, sitting on the sofa. He'd been in her apartment several times when they'd been dating. She looked away, wishing she wasn't remembering those dates. Those kisses. That wild and wonderful night.

"Now is not a good time. You can see my mother's visiting." Mitzie walked by and Anna leaned over and scooped her up, glad to have something to do. Tanner made her nervous.

"Unexpectedly?" he asked.

"Very. And she hasn't a clue who you are except of course CEO of Drysdale. I don't want her to know. At least not until we know how we're going to handle things."

Tanner settled back in the cushions, his eyes narrowed slightly. "And why is that?"

"My mother's old-fashioned and would think that the man who got me pregnant should marry me to give the baby a name. That would sure play havoc with your I-don't-want-to-marry stance, wouldn't it? I don't want her to know yet."

"The whole world will know sooner or later," he said.

"Not if I don't tell anyone. I could say it was a one-night stand, which come to think about it, it was."

"It was not."

"We only did it once, Tanner, what would you call it?"

"The culmination of a great relationship."

"Which you ended quick enough after that night." Even known the reasons, she couldn't entirely get rid of the hurt his defection had caused.

"Because I found out you worked for Drysdale and I knew I'd be taking that company over," he said again.

"Still, it was only once," she repeated stubbornly.

"I'm sorry I hurt you, Anna, it wasn't my intention," he said softly.

She refused to look at him. She tried to ignore the ache in her heart that had been there since he had stopped returning her calls, stopped calling her. She had thought he was so special, and he'd only been looking for a casual dating partner. She ran her hands down Mitzie's soft fur.

Tanner leaned forward, reaching for Anna's hand. "It wasn't a one-night stand. There's a difference between that and only making love one time."

"Like we're going to do it again?" she asked.

"The situation surrounding the baby will surface sooner or later," he said, rubbing his thumb over the back of her hand.

The motion was mesmerizing. She could feel her insides warming up. Snatching her hand away, she pushed the chair back a few inches, trying to put distance between them. How could she still be susceptible to the man?

"We need to decide what we're going to do about it," he said.

"You must have decided…you sure contacted an attorney fast enough. I saw one today. And she gave me lots of papers to look over, which present different options. I'll try to see if we can work something out if your parents want a relationship with this grandchild."

"What if I want a relationship with this child?" he asked.

She looked at him in amazement. It was the last thing she expected. And would that complicate matters!

"You won't see much of the baby when I'm living in Brussels," she said slowly, her heart beating faster. What if he put roadblocks in her way? Would he really want a relationship is this child?

"So maybe you don't move to Brussels."

Anna felt as if she'd been slapped. She glared at him. "I have worked long and hard for that promotion. You can't deny it."

He shrugged, his eyes glinting. "Actually I could rescind the promotion."

"Don't you dare talk like that. Besides I would think you'd be glad to have the embarrassment several thousand miles away rather than in the same office day after day."

"What embarrassment?"

"That your lover is having your baby and still hanging around."

"So you're the father of the baby," Ginny said from the kitchen door.

Anna turned to her mother in horror.

"Mom! I didn't want you to know. We're still working things out," she said.

"Seems to me the only thing needed to be worked out is how soon he will marry you," Ginny said as she glared at Tanner.

"Marriage is not an option," Anna said quickly.

Tanner looked at her and frowned. "Are you speaking for me now?" he asked.

She looked back at him. "Come on, Tanner, you know that's the last thing you want. You've already accused me of trying to trap you. You should be celebrating that I am not." She dumped the cat off her lap and stood.

Ginny looked at Tanner. "What do your parents think?"

He looked startled for a moment. "A good question. I haven't told them the news yet."

"It's too soon to tell anybody," Anna said desperately. "The doctor didn't guarantee I'll carry this child to full-term. I don't want anyone else to know yet. I couldn't bear all the sympathy if I lose the baby before it's born."

Tanner rose. "I believe this is something that Anna and I need to discuss on our own," he said politely to her mother. Turning to her he said, "Maybe after dinner you'd feel up to a walk."

No way!

"Maybe another day. I'm tired and I have a lot to think about after visiting the attorney this afternoon," she said. She was hardly dressed to go for a walk, and didn't feel up to changing to suit Tanner.

He glanced at the packet of papers on the sofa. "You may have a lot to review but don't even think about making any decisions without talking to me. I have a hectic week. Tonight was the only time I had available. I'll come by at ten o'clock on Saturday morning. We can talk then." He said good-night and left the apartment.

Anna gazed at the closed door for a number of moments. She had to face her mother. She so wished things had not come to this.

"We don't want to get married, Mom," she said. Anna marveled at the even tone of her voice. For a second she wondered what it would be like to marry Tanner, to spend the pregnancy together anticipating the baby's birth. Deciding what to name the child, how to decorate the nursery.

She shook her head as if dislodging the image. She was fine on her own.

"How can you say that? You made a baby with this man," her mother said.

"Ever since Jason canceled our engagement I stopped thinking about getting married. I figured nobody would want me despite all your urging to forget Jason and move on. I don't want to be caught up in love like I was only to lose it all. God that hurt so much. It's safer to keep away from entanglements. Tanner and I had a great time this summer. We seemed to click on so many levels, from shared values to liking the same kind of movies and books. Our tastes in music differed but that made things interesting. Then without warning he stopped calling, stopped returning my calls. I know now it was because he found out I worked for the company he was taking over and he did not want personal lives mixed with business."

Anna agreed philosophically with his decision, but in her heart, she wished he'd continued to call. She could have kept the relationships separate. Or at the very least she wished that he had explained.

"It's not right," Ginny said stubbornly.

"Let's eat dinner. Then I could use a good night's sleep. How long are you staying?" Anna asked, firmly changing the subject.

Her mother led the way back into the kitchen to dish up. "Until tomorrow. You know your father doesn't like doing things on his own. With all you children grown there's nobody else to do things for him but me. So I need to get back home."

"Are you happy being married to Daddy?" Anna asked when they were seated at the table, plates piled high with spaghetti.

"What a question!" Ginny said.

"You never worked outside the home. You never had a career except being a mom to your kids and a wife to Daddy. I just wondered—is it enough?"

"It was my choice and for me it's been enough. Now I get to spend time with my grandkids. For some people maybe they'd want more. It probably would not be enough for you who likes her job so much. Or have you used it as a substitute for getting a family?"

Anna gazed off dreamily. "Before when I

thought I couldn't get pregnant it was my only option—it wasn't a choice. Now, I wonder what it would be like to stay home with my baby. Watch it grow from a tiny infant into a rambunctious toddler. See it learn, be fascinated by the world. It sounds fun on the one hand, but I've been so consumed with my work, I feel I couldn't make it just talking to a baby all day. Am I wrong in wanting to combine both career and motherhood?"

"Not wrong, just your choice. I made different ones. But you are not superwoman. Some things will have to change. You don't just add a baby to the mix and go on the way you've been doing."

"I know that already and have only known I'm pregnant for a week. I'm cutting back on the hours I work. I'll manage."

"I want you to more than manage. I want you to thrive."

Anna smiled. "I'm glad you came, Mom. Tell me more of what I can expect as this baby develops."

Her mother left for home early the next morning. Anna enjoyed visiting with her mother. They had talked far into the night about what having a baby would entail.

Anna went to work not knowing what to expect from Tanner. She felt let down as the day progressed and Tanner never called her or asked to see her. She tried to tell herself she was fine with that. She had lots to catch up on. But she was annoyed he seemed to compartmentalize his life when she was so focused on the coming baby and the connection with its father. Yet, he had told her this week would be hectic.

Anna went to work each day, did her best and came home early to rest. She took time to review all the material that the attorney had given her. She also read two of her books on being pregnant and caring for a newborn. She was in bed each night by eight, and often thought of Tanner before falling asleep.

Saturday morning she rose early to make sure her apartment was spotless before Tanner arrived. She didn't know if he'd want to come inside before going for another walk. But cleaning kept her busy and not fretting about the coming confrontation.

Promptly at ten Tanner rang her doorbell. She opened a couple of seconds later. He wore dark chords and a sweater. "It's cold out," he said. "Dress warmly. I think a brisk walk is in order."

"Easier to talk when walking than face-to-face?" she asked.

"Right. Plus, it puts us in neutral territory."

So he did see them as adversaries. Would he listen to her suggestions or try to ride roughshod over them to get his own way?

She put on her jacket, a warm hat and gloves. She felt as nervous as if on a first date. She remembered the other walks they'd taken. One of the things they enjoyed together—long rambling walks around the city when the crowds were no longer there. It was even better this time of year when most tourists were gone.

But this was not another fun date. This was a serious discussion to determine the future for the child they had created.

"So where do we start?" she asked as they headed down the hill toward the Bay. The wind blew cold. She could see her breath. The exertion felt good.

"Maybe we start with custody," Tanner said.

She looked at him in surprise. "You mean you'd challenge my custody of my own baby?" She couldn't keep the astonishment out of her voice.

"Maybe. Remember, Anna, it's not just your baby, it's as much mine. I vote for shared custody."

"And that would work how?" she asked. It felt odd to discuss the baby as if it were a commodity. She wasn't sure she was going to be able to treat it so cavalierly once it was born. It would be tiny, dependent on her for love and care and comfort. Could she share with Tanner, no matter what legal documents said?

"We draw up papers, agree to the terms and once the baby is born, you have him, or her, several days a week, I get the baby the other days."

"Why would you even consider doing such a thing?" she asked. She hated the idea. He was approaching this like a business deal!

"I take it you haven't thought it through," he said.

"Not at all." She wasn't sure she wanted to give up any control of her baby. In only two months, she'd be in Brussels. A custody arrangement could derail that option.

"I have thought about it, a lot. There was an—" he hesitated for a long moment "—incident when I was younger. Hell, more than that. Anna, I had a son. Then I didn't. There was nothing I could do about that. This time I can and will do something. I'm not going through that pain again."

"Oh, Tanner, I'm so sorry! I never knew you had a child before. How sad to lose a baby." For a moment the knowledge almost brought her to tears. She knew how she'd grieve if she was unable to bring this baby to term. How much worse would a parent feel if he or she lost a baby to death once they'd held the precious child in their arms?

She reached out and covered his hand with hers. "I am so sorry."

"I don't want a similar situation," he said, his eyes hard, his expression fierce, as if pushing away any sentimentality. Tanner looked like the ruthless businessman he was reputed to be.

"I'm thinking about my parents, too. They loved Zach. They were as devastated as I when he left," he said.

"Left?" Was that the euphemism he used for death—to make it easier to deal with?

Tanner studied her for a long moment. They paused at the light—when the signal changed, they began walking again, crossing the street.

"When I was finishing college, I met a girl, Cindy. We clicked immediately and before I knew it, she was pregnant. We got married and had a baby boy—Zachary." For a moment Tanner looked away, letting his gaze roam ahead of them. Whitecaps could be seen on the water in the distance. Sailboats dotted the expanse. Then he looked back at Anna.

"When he was just over a year Cindy told me Zach wasn't mine. She'd had a falling out with her boyfriend and had rebounded with me. The other man was back and he wanted Cindy and his baby. I fought it, but the DNA test proved the baby was his. I had no recourse but to divorce her and let them go. I never saw either of them again."

Anna stopped and stared at him, her heart heavy with his story. It wasn't as final as death, but the result was the same. Tanner never saw his baby boy again.

Then she thought it through. Panic flared. She was not giving up her baby to anyone—even its father.

"I'm sorry about Zach. I can see why you want some assurance that you'll be a part of this baby's life," she began.

"I want all parental rights to this child. If I have to fight for them, I will," Tanner said, his eyes dark and hard.

"You don't need to fight. I thought you wouldn't want to be tied down. Of course you can have time with your baby." She bit her lip. "But as an infant, he won't be much company. He'll need care and nurturing and his mother."

"I want to spend time at all stages until I am an old man and die. Do you know what it's like to love a child and have him snatched away and never even hear about him? I don't know if that man is a good father to him. If Zach is happy. Does he like sports, or is he more scientific? Does he do well in school or is it a struggle? Is he as tall as I am now or still a gawky in between stage? I don't know and I never will."

She could hear the pain in his voice. For a

moment the full ramifications of their act hit her. They had made a baby together and forever would be tied to each other through their child. They both wanted the baby, and wanted the best for him or her. Yet fear coursed through her. She wanted to be with her child. She couldn't bear the thought of Tanner fighting her for custody.

"So if I go to Brussels, the baby will live thousands of miles from San Francisco," she said. Would that provide a layer of safety?

He took a deep breath. "The Brussels assignment is up in the air. I want to be with you when the baby is born."

Anna stared at him in dismay. "We don't have that kind of relationship. We ended things, right? You did. I have made plans."

"You'll need to change them. I'm changing my plans for the future for the sake of the baby, you'll have to as well."

"But I'm moving in January. I've been planning for this opportunity for years. Over ten years, Tanner. You can't take that away. I've worked hard for the promotion. It's already been promised."

"I'm not taking anything away, just postponing. Think about it a minute. You're going to be having your first child at age thirty-eight. You're going to want your mother there. You'll want to share this baby with your family and friends. I sure want my parents to know this baby, to love him or her. I want to be there—to bond with my child. And to know he can never be taken away from me. Living in Belgium would create a hardship for everybody. Not to mention I think it'd be a hardship on you having to do everything on your own without family and friends around. If you wait until the baby is a year or two old—"

"A year or two? I thought you just said until the baby was born." Anna was growing more upset. Her longed-for promotion looked as if it were going up in flames.

"Let me finish. Once the baby's old enough to attend a good day care it would be easier for you to make that move."

"And who decides that? You?"

He nodded. "Maybe. I'll want liberal visitation rights throughout the child's life. Maybe even joint custody. I'm not giving up this baby!"

"I don't like it. All the benefits seem to be on your side. What do I get—a delay in my promotion, maybe the chance will fall altogether. Most people want a permanent job, not one as a place holder while I take time out to have a baby."

What she was also afraid of was that she could grow to like the suggestion. She *would* like to be near her mother when the baby was born. She did want her sister and brother and their families to get to know her child and for the child to be loved by everyone. And the baby would enable her to spend more time with Tanner.

Though how hard would that be? Wanting to develop some kind of deeper relationship and only be together because of a baby? A clean break would be easier. But it didn't look as if anything about this pregnancy was going to be easy.

What would it be like to have Tanner spend the baby's formative months sharing in its growth and development? What exactly did he envision? Everybody would rejoice to have her stay—except her.

She had dreams. A future to build and secure for her child. What of Eurpoe?

"I don't know that's the best solution," she said slowly. She turned and began walking again. There were so many decisions to make. She felt pressured. Why couldn't he give her a chance to come to terms with the life-changing event. Give her time to think everything through and make some decisions for the best of all?

Passing a coffee shop, Tanner reached out and took her arm gently.

"Let's get something to drink. It's colder than I thought and your face is rosy from the cold. We'll discuss the ramifications and see if we can come to an agreement."

Did he really wish to be there when the baby was born? She hadn't thought about the actual birth. What kind of father would Tanner prove to be? Patient and tolerant? It sounded like he wanted a hands-on kind of parenting. Would he attend school plays and sports events? She'd see him all the time.

She found a table to one side while Tanner went to get their beverages. Watching him, Anna remembered how much fun they had last summer. How unhappy she'd been when he stopped calling. She wished nothing had changed—and yet everything had changed. He wouldn't be with her today if she wasn't pregnant. Not much of a recommendation for deepening a relationship.

Tanner stood in the short line and glanced over his shoulder at Anna. Her eyes met his before she quickly looked away. He wished he could read her mind. He'd talked with his attorney twice to get his input and further suggestions. He'd spoken the truth when he said he wanted this baby. After the initial shock he had to admit he was excited about another child. He'd missed so much of Zach's life. Would he be able to change things with this child? Spend enough time with him or her as a live-out father? Really be a part of the baby's life?

Not if Anna took off for Brussels.

That was the first hurdle to overcome. He had to get her to change her mind. To remain in San Francisco until after the baby was born. What could he say to convince her?

And in the meantime what would they do with the European Division? He could ask Thomas to postpone his retirement or he could hire somebody on an interim basis. Or flat out give the job to somebody else.

Anna would kill him if he did that. But he'd do it in a heartbeat if it meant keeping her here.

If he hadn't taken on the CEO position at Drysdale Electronic they'd probably still be seeing each other. How would he have taken the news of her pregnancy? Probably just as badly in light of her pending move.

He paid for their beverages and walked to the table she chose, placing the mugs on the table and sitting opposite her. Anna took her cup and sipped.

"Caffeine free," he said, raising his cup in toast.

"Thank you."

"How do you feel?" he asked.

"I feel much better this week than last."

Tanner studied her as she talked. She may say she was better, but she still looked pale. What of that myth that women glowed in pregnancy?

God, he couldn't believe he'd gotten her pregnant.

He'd never thought to marry again after Cindy's perfidy. Never expected to have another child. A baby was a hostage to the future. So many things could go wrong. How did parents risk it time and time again? Now that there was nothing to be done, he was resigned to the situation. Resigned and excited. He had to convince Anna to stay.

"So let's work out an agreement that suits both, sign a contract and get going," he said.

She shook her head. "It's not that easy."

"Sure it is. We just do it."

She sighed softly and sipped her coffee, glancing around the coffee shop at the other couples talking, laughing.

Tears welled in her eyes and for a moment Tanner felt a punch of panic. She wasn't going to cry was she?

"Tanner, I've worked so hard for this chance at the position in Europe. Yet all I ever thought about when my sister was rejoicing in her pregnancies, or my brother's wife was pregnant, was how much I wished I could have a baby. I don't know what to do. I want this baby, but what if I can't do my job because I'm needed for the baby? Or what if I can't deliver? My doctor says he doesn't want to frighten me, but with appointments every week and cautionary suggestions, how can I help but be afraid I won't deliver a healthy infant?"

"Women have babies and work all the time. And the job will wait for you, Anna. We both made this baby. Let me help you until you're ready to go to Brussels."

"I'm ready now."

"After the baby is born. Let me be there when it's born. Let me share in its life."

Tanner knew he was being a bit reckless. But surprisingly he trusted Anna and wanted to do what he could to put her at ease with the situation. She was not Cindy. He had to remember that. The situation was totally different. There was no question this was his child.

"I don't know."

He felt a flare of triumph. She sounded as if she was weakening. The next step—coming up with a legal agreement. She was no longer putting up barriers.

"You're moving too fast," she said.

"The next months will fly by. We don't have a lot of time to waste," he said.

He leaned over and brushed back the locks of hair that had drifted across her cheek. "We enjoyed each other's company last summer. Let's remember that and recapture some of those feelings while we're together. Neither of us wants forever. It would be a good thing if the time we spend together is enjoyable. We had something special, Anna. Let's recapture that."

CHAPTER SIX

TANNER was still trying to wrap his mind around the idea of becoming a father again. With a difference this time—he knew the baby was his. No one was taking it away from him.

For a moment the memory of their night together flashed into his mind. It had been incredible. Anna had been loving and wild in bed and about driven him up the wall with desire. They'd made love several times during the night. He'd hated to leave in the morning, which in itself was unusual. He preferred to skip the awkwardness of the morning after. But it hadn't been awkward with Anna.

That had come when he stopped calling her.

He was well past the age where he hopped into bed with anybody who caught his eye. He'd focused on his business career after Cindy left, rising rapidly in the corporate world. Late summer had been the most fun he had outside of business in a long time.

What would it be like to spend more time with

Anna? To share a child together? To keep a connection down through the years?

"This is important to me, and I want you to think seriously about it. Let's give our baby every chance we can," he said.

Anna regarded him steadily. After a long moment she dropped her gaze and took another sip of her coffee. Tanner wished again that he could read her mind. Her posture indicated resistance. How ironic. Wasn't it usually the man doing the protesting? Instead he was doing all he could to convince her it was the right decision.

"I still don't think it's a good idea," she said so softly Tanner almost didn't hear her.

"If you've got a better idea, now's the time to bring it up."

"We could just go on the way we have been," she offered.

"Not an option," he said flatly. If it weren't so ironic, he could see the humor in the situation. He had married Cindy thinking she was pregnant with his baby when she was not. Now he'd not brought up the subject of marriage with Anna—who definitely was pregnant with his baby. Should he?

They sat in silence. Anna sipped her coffee, gazed around at the other people in the coffee shop. Tanner kept his eyes deliberately on her. If he had to, he would force the issue.

As if sensing his resolve, she looked at him again. "So at what point would you think the baby ready to move to Brussels?" she asked.

"I don't know, but certainly not before it was several months old."

For the first time he began to think of what it would be like to be involved with a baby again. She'd need help when it was a newborn. Babies only slept a few hours at a time. It took a team to handle that aspect. Would she breast-feed or bottle feed? Cindy had bottle fed and he relished the nights he'd taken turns to feed Zach. He'd made such plans for the boy's life during those small hours in the morning.

He remembered the surprising joy he felt at each milestone. No matter that he was from another man, Tanner would forever think of Zachary as his son. He missed him every day.

"So which attorney drafts a formal agreement?" she asked.

Tanner felt elated. She was going to acquiesce.

"If it makes you feel better, have your attorney draft it. I'll have mine review it and once we are in accord we sign."

Anna didn't look happy. "This is not what I ever pictured having a baby would be like," she said sadly.

He shrugged. "We do our best with the cards we're dealt."

She nodded slowly. "If we're really going to do this, then I think you need to meet my family at some point. I'm telling them about the baby at Thanksgiving."

Tanner shrugged. "If you think they'll want to meet me. They aren't going to be too happy with the situation, do you think?"

Anna shook her head, pushing her coffee cup away. "Not especially. I think they'll be happy for me. Probably not so happy the way things came about. But I've been on my own for a lot of years. I'll try to cover everything with my attorney. I want to go home now."

Tanner looked at her sharply. "Are you feeling well?"

"I'm tired, I want to go home."

As they walked back to Anna's apartment, Tanner had mixed emotions. He knew this was the right thing to do, but wished Anna had been more open to the idea.

When they reached her apartment building, Anna turned at the entry. "We can make this work, right?" she asked.

"We can make it anything we want," he said. Unable to stop himself, he reached up to brush strands of hair that were flying in the breeze, tucking some of them behind her ear. Her skin was soft and cool. Her cheeks rosy from the coldness. Her eyes looked sad. Leaning closer Tanner kissed her briefly.

"We will make this work, Anna."

"It's just so different than I ever imagined," she said.

"Different maybe, that doesn't mean it's bad. Go on up and get some rest."

Anna called her attorney first thing Monday morning and asked for another appointment. It was hard to concentrate on work when she knew she would not be moving to Brussels in a couple of months as planned. In fact, it was likely to be much more than a year before she would leave. For a moment the thought of losing her coveted position brought sadness. If she could not carry this baby to term she would need the challenges of the European operation to take her mind off her loss.

But what if she did carry the baby to term? She had never expected to become pregnant. Would she care at all about the delay moving to Brussels when she held her precious infant in her arms? Then she'd probably be glad to have her mother nearby, have her brother and sister and their families get to know her baby. But it was as if she was letting go of one life—without knowing if she would have the chance of a new one.

Her attorney discussed the details of the agreement, offering suggestions when Anna had no definite idea of the limits she wanted to impose. Legally she had no recourse to deny him equal access to the child. She'd thought about it during the weekend, putting herself in his position.

She would not want to be deprived of a minute of being with her child. And Tanner had to feel doubly wary after losing Zachary so finally.

When they'd hashed out all details, Jillian agreed to draw up an agreement given the parameters they'd discussed. She promised to have it ready within a week to send to Tanner's attorney.

Anna walked back to Drysdale Electronics. The weather was cloudy, rain was forecast, but for the moment, it was merely overcast. She hoped Tanner would agree to all the terms. It had been hard planning for holidays and school breaks when the baby wasn't even born. But Jillian had been thorough.

Anna passed one of the restaurants she and Tanner had previously eaten at. She'd been consumed by him then, thrilled every time he asked her out. Reliving every date when she'd go to bed each night. They'd had so much in common, she'd been fast falling for the man, tossing aside her stringent rules about not risking her heart. Would she have tumbled the rest of the way if they'd seen each other longer? How fortuitous he'd ended things when he had in light of the changes.

She wished Tanner had never taken a job at Drysdale Electronic. Maybe she should wish he had not tried out the new gym before he took on the role of CEO.

But did she wish she'd never met him?

Not for an instant.

If not for Tanner, she would not be expecting a baby in seven months.

Tanner clicked on the television to watch the football game. It had been a frenetic week with the last of the reorganization he wanted to get behind him. The company was structured now the way he saw it functioning best. He'd hired a couple of men he knew could deliver the kind of results he wanted. He was holding a watching brief on one other manager. The man sounded good, talked a good line, but Tanner had an uneasy feeling about him. Still, he was giving him the benefit of the doubt for the time being.

With those hard changes made, he could settle

in now and concentrate on the day-to-day running of the firm.

This weekend he was taking some downtime. He had only seen Anna during the week at a distance. He'd spoken to Thomas in Brussels and surprised the man when he'd asked him to consider remaining in the job a little longer. Thomas was getting back to Tanner next week with his answer.

The only other major hurtle was letting his parents know of their coming grandchild.

He hesitated to call. Not because he didn't think they'd be thrilled. They had been devastated when Cindy broke the truth and took Zach away. They'd adored their grandchild and had hoped for many more.

This time there would be no taking away once the baby was born.

For the first time since he'd learned the news, Tanner stopped to consider the admonition Anna had given. *She might not deliver a full-term baby.*

He'd been so caught up with the fight to keep his child nearby, he'd neglected to pay attention to her cautionary words. Was she in danger? Or only the baby?

He could envision a baby with curly hair and bright blue eyes gazing up adoringly at her mother. For a moment Tanner felt a pang that this

was not a real family. A forever family. He suspected going into this arrangement that there
would be no happy-ever-after. They would share
the birth of their child and its formative years. But
Anna had other challenges to conquer and he'd
forged his own future long ago. They'd go their
separate ways with only their son or daughter as
a link between them. The thought made him sad.

He stared at the television, not seeing the
players. What would his life be like with a child?
He'd have to arrange for help while the baby was
young. He wouldn't be able to take off work every
time it came to stay with him.

How did Anna plan to handle things? Maybe
they should hire a nanny between them, and have
the nanny accompany the baby at whichever place
it was staying. Dare he suggest that to her?

The doorbell rang. He went to the door, surprised to find Anna there.

"I hope I'm not intruding," she said, peering
beyond him into the empty living room.

"You're not. Come in." He stood to one side.
She had not been in his apartment before. How
had she found out where he lived?

"I got the papers from my attorney. She sent a
set to yours, but I thought you might like to see
what's what."

He closed the door behind her and took her

jacket. Anna looked around the apartment and walked over to the sofa, glancing at the television.

"If this is not a good time, I can just leave the papers."

"Now is fine." He used the remote to turn off the TV. He held his hand out for the envelope and quickly withdrew the small packet of papers.

"Want something to drink?" he asked, already beginning to read the document.

"No."

Tanner sat at the end of the sofa and quickly skimmed the top sheet. The document was not in complete legalese; he could understand the terms clearly.

When he finished, he looked up.

"Satisfied?" she asked.

"For the most part." It was a fair document. Whether Anna's ideas or those of her attorney's he didn't know, or care. He could live with the terms as proposed. At least initially. Maybe they'd wish to alter things as the child grew, but that was a decision to make when the time came.

"So we see how it goes," he said.

"Why are you doing this, Tanner?"

He could be no less than honest. "I'll admit to being selfish, Anna. I see this chance to watch my second child grow and be able to share all the milestones I missed with Zach. I don't want to wake up one morning and find you and the baby gone and not know where you are, not have time I know I can count on to spend with my child."

"And what about my plans? Do you know how long I've been planning to move to Europe?"

"Europe will be there. A baby moves through different stages so fast if you blink you'll miss them," he said.

"If you agree to the points I proposed, I guess the attorneys can handle things from now on," she said.

"You make it sound like we won't see each other again."

She shrugged. "You're the one who called a halt to our dating. Now that I work for you, I can see your point. Office romances can get sticky."

He tossed the papers into the space between them. "On the other hand, we'd know where we stand. And we have a common goal—deliver a healthy baby. Maybe I should revisit that decision."

Anna was surprised at Tanner's statement. It was the last thing she'd expected. He would change his long-held stance—just because of the baby?

"You look surprised," he said.

"I am."

"Why? You'll need someone to help you—doctor visits, buying furniture, getting things for an infant. Who better than the father? Won't you want me to accompany you to the doctor? At least for the ultrasound? And what about a birthing partner?"

She stared at him. He sounded as if he wanted to be with her every step of the way. This did not fit her picture of Tanner as ruthless businessman at all.

"There's no one else, right?" he asked.

She shook her head.

"I always wondered why not last summer," he said.

"Why not what?" Anna asked, still trying to wrap her mind around the idea of his accompanying her to the doctor. Of his presence at the ultrasound or other exams. She could feel the flush of embarrassment steal into her cheeks.

"Why haven't you married? I remember once you said you had been engaged. What happened?"

"Unlike you, who never said anything and who had been married." She didn't like to talk about Jason.

"So I learned young that marriage isn't for me. But most women seem to want to be married."

"And some prefer a career."

"I hadn't heard the two were mutually exclusive," he said dryly. "Most of the women at Drysdale are married, aren't they? And each has a career."

"I was engaged once," she said slowly. She rarely talked about Jason. What was the point? But Tanner had shared his past, she could do no less.

"What happened?" he asked.

"We were making plans for where we would live after we married and Jason said something about wanting a big house and yard for the children. We had never discussed that before— he'd never said anything about wanting children. I had to tell him I couldn't have a baby. He went really still, then got up and left. The next day he came to see me to tell me he wanted children—his children. If I couldn't provide them, it was better we called it quits at that point rather than later."

"Bastard."

"A lot of men want their own children."

"A woman isn't solely a baby machine," Tanner said. He rose and paced to the window. "So did he go on to marry and have a bunch of kids?"

"I don't know what happened to him after we split." She had never tried to find out. Her sister had urged her to do so at one time—just to bring some kind of closure, but Anna felt she had all the closure she needed. Bottom line—she'd not been good enough for Jason Donalds.

Only—it turned out she might have been. If they'd gotten married, would she eventually have become pregnant?

For a moment she daydreamed of finding Jason and casually walking by him at a store or the mall, pushing her baby in a carriage.

But of course, he'd fallen out of love with her as she had with him, so there would be no emotional elation on showing him she could have a baby.

And there were no guarantees she was going to deliver a healthy infant. The daydream vanished. The niggling worry returned. She was able to push it away for long periods of time, but it slipped in when she was not expecting it.

"How far do you want to take this seeing each other bit," she asked.

He turned and leaned against the wall, his hands in his pants pockets.

"As in?"

"I have a doctor's appointment every Tuesday afternoon. I was able to make them at five, so I only have to leave work a little early. I don't want to cause any gossip until I have a better feel for whether this little one is going to be okay. I'm scheduled for a sonogram next week, and then I'll have another later in the pregnancy."

If there was a later. But she didn't reveal that fear to Tanner. She tried to keep those thoughts at bay. She wanted this baby so much. She didn't know what she'd do if she lost it.

"I'll make arrangements to go with you next week. And whenever I can thereafter," Tanner said.

"Are you serious about being there at the delivery?" She hadn't thought that far ahead. Some of it was superstition. If she didn't count on anything, maybe she wouldn't be disappointed.

"Why not? I was there at the conception. I like to see a project through."

She almost smiled at his attempt at humor. But the magnitude of the situation wasn't funny.

"You'll have to meet my parents. You met my mom, but not under the best circumstances."

"And how have things improved?" he asked.

She did smile at that. "They haven't, but you still need to meet my family. They'll want to know the father of my baby."

The more she thought about it, the more it seemed Brussels was farther and farther away.

On the other hand, if she stayed in San Francisco to have her baby and for a few months after, maybe it would be for the best. She'd be surrounded by friends and her family wasn't that far away. And the baby's daddy would be close by as well.

If she carried it to term. She constantly reminded herself of that. She still couldn't believe in the miracle and expected something horrible to happen before the due date. She shivered, hoping against hope she'd one day hold her baby.

She couldn't think about that. She looked at Tanner. "Come and spend Thanksgiving Day with my family."

He considered the idea. She watched him remembering how much she'd enjoyed spending time with him. He still had the power to stop her heart with his good looks. She loved the way he'd look at her as if she were the only other person in the world. His dark eyes could melt her bones. She wished she still had the right to run her fingers through his hair, feel its texture, the warmth of his skin against her palm and fingertips. Feel his mouth on hers again. Would they ever make love again? She grew warm just thinking about it.

"A simple yes or no would suffice," she said once she realized he hadn't answered.

"A bit awkward, don't you think?"

"They have to be hospitable if you visit. It's only for dinner. They live in Stockton. It's about a three-hour drive. My parents have always held dinner at one o'clock on Thanksgiving. So we could drive over in the morning, eat, and drive back."

"No. That's a family day. I'd be in the way. And it would be awkward, if not worse. There will be time enough to meet them before the baby comes," he said.

Anna didn't blame him. She knew she'd refuse if he invited her to a holiday event with his family. They weren't that close.

And the thought made her sad. For a few glorious weeks she'd been caught up in the delight of getting to know this man, to feeling the symptoms of falling in love. She relished being part of a couple, of making plans together.

It was all gone now.

"Will they make things difficult for you?" he asked.

"I don't see how. If you only knew how much I wanted a baby over the years, how everyone thought it would never happen, I think they'll be happy for me."

"But that does bring up the question of marriage."

"No, it doesn't."

"Do you want me to marry you for the sake of the baby?" Tanner asked.

Anna felt her heart jump. For a split second— wait, what had he said? For the sake of the baby?

No, she didn't want to marry anyone for such a reason.

She shook her head and rose. "No, I don't want to marry you for the baby. It'll be fine with me as a single mom. I have to go."

"Stay for a while," Tanner said, moving away

from the window. "What else are you going to do today?"

"Take a nap after lunch," she said, inching toward the door. She really didn't want to stay. His comment about marriage had her suddenly longing for the very thing. Only not because of a baby, but for love and devotion and a longing to share her life with someone. Could she find someone to love, to share her life with?

Not likely. The sooner she nipped that notion, the better.

He walked over to the door, snagging her jacket as he passed the chair. "Thanks for bringing the papers by. I'll look over them carefully and let you know if I want anything different."

"Fine."

He helped her put the jacket on, brushing the back of his fingers against her cheek and leaned closer until Anna held her breath. Was he going to kiss her again?

He did. Not just a brush against her lips, but a full-blown kiss, the kind they'd shared last summer. The kind she'd yearned for during the weeks she hadn't seen him. The kind she never thought she'd have again.

She was almost breathless when he lifted his head.

"Need a ride home?"

"No, I'm good. Bye." She opened the door and almost ran out of his apartment. Her heart was racing, her blood zinging through her body. She felt exhilarated, more alive than she had in weeks. Oh, oh, she was in trouble.

Anna chose to walk home, both for the exercise and to get some control over her emotions. She couldn't believe Tanner wanted to play such an active part in the baby's life. Yet how could she deny the man time with his child? Especially when she knew he grieved the loss of that first baby he thought was his. She'd have to find a way to deal with the emotions he evoked. No more kisses.

When she reached her place, she fixed lunch and then called her mother.

After the preliminaries were out of the way, she broached the subject, "I thought I'd finalize plans for Thanksgiving. I'll be down that morning and stay until Sunday."

"How are you feeling?"

"Much better now. Almost back to normal, except I'm tired all the time."

"And the baby's father?"

Anna hesitated, not sure how much to tell her mother.

"He wants an active role in the child's life. We

are already discussing custody arrangements." It sounded so odd. She felt a pang. She didn't want to share this baby with anyone. Yet at some point she might have to split each week

"I plan to tell everyone I'm pregnant when we're all together. That'll work, won't it?" Anna wanted to share her good news. Maybe if she told everyone, nothing bad would happen. She'd have a textbook perfect pregnancy and deliver a healthy, beautiful baby.

She wasn't quite sure how her sister and brother would take the news. She knew they'd be happy for her, but probably question the wisdom of bringing the baby in the world as a single woman. But her family would only be critical because they loved her. She had to make sure they knew this is exactly what she wanted. This was so complicated.

"Best time to tell them. We can all make plans if we're together. I can't wait to hold that new baby!"

After she finished talking with her mother, she went to take that nap. The luxury of the weekend was the ability to sleep as much as she wanted. She needed to rest up—the weekdays were hectic.

Feeling refreshed when she awoke, Anna wandered into the living room and began to review some notes from work. It was late afternoon when the telephone rang. She was surprised to hear Tanner's voice when she picked up.

"Do you want to have dinner with me?" he asked.

Anna hesitated a moment. Being with him wasn't the same as it had been last summer. Then they had plenty to talk about. Now it seemed everything revolved around the baby. She was afraid to say too much for fear of rocking the boat.

"It's only dinner, Anna."

"Okay, then. Thanks."

"We should plan our strategy," he said. "How about I pick up some Chinese food and come to your place?"

"That sounds fine."

She sat on the sofa for a long moment after she hung up wondering if she could rediscover some of the camaraderie they had enjoyed last summer. She didn't want to only talk about the baby. She wanted to have fun with Tanner. Was that lost forever?

CHAPTER SEVEN

TANNER hung up the phone. Anna's reception had been less than what he'd hoped for. She seemed distant and aloof. Of course his initial thoughtless ending of their relationship hadn't helped. And then his accusation that she was trying to trap him in some way had furthered the rift.

Still, he had asked her if she wanted to get married. He still didn't know if he was relieved she'd refused, or a bit disappointed.

Which made no sense. He wasn't going down that road again. Once had been enough.

Though he was sure putting himself at risk becoming involved with this baby. He still missed Zach. But how could he not want to know this child? He'd loved little Zach with a fierceness that surprised him. The loss had been almost more than he could bear. None of his friends understood. Most thought he should be glad to be out from under the responsibility of a child. Especially one that biologically wasn't his.

But Tanner had never felt that for a second.

He rose and went to get his wallet. He'd pick up Chinese food and see if they could come to some sort of truce. He didn't want Anna acting jumpy and skittish around him. As far as he was concerned, the entire world could think what it wanted. It was nobody's business but their own that they planed a temporary alliance until the birth of their child. This time business would have to take second place.

He called ahead and the dinner was ready when he arrived at the restaurant they had frequented last summer. He knew the dishes she favored. There was work waiting to be done back at his apartment. He had to get into the office early tomorrow. But he wanted this time with Anna.

Tanner was struck by how pretty she looked when she opened the door. She was wearing the same casual slacks and a loose-fitting top she'd had on that morning. Her hair hung around her shoulders soft and wavy. Her eyes looked bright and there was faint color in her cheeks.

For one blinding moment he wanted to sweep her into his arms and kiss her till she didn't know her own name, then take her to bed. Gritting his teeth against that urge, he held up the white paper bag.

"I got everything you liked," he said, banishing the image.

"I hope you got something you like, too," she said.

"Sure."

She stepped aside and he entered her apartment. In only moments she had plates on the dining room table and they were opening the various cartons of food.

Once they began to eat, he broached the subject, "We need to talk about how to present this to the world," Tanner said. "Once you tell your family, and I tell mine, there's no reason to keep it a secret."

"The thing is, Tanner, I hate for everyone to think this baby came as a result of a one-night stand. I'd rather they thought we were at least attracted to each other and as a result the baby came to be, rather than they learn the truth."

He frowned and didn't say anything for a few moments. He studied Anna for a moment. He realized he didn't like the thought, either, that people would think they'd just made love once. He wanted more for Anna. And for himself. He wanted to be a part of her life. Not for the baby, but for himself. The thought shocked him. Was he thinking long-term?

"So what do you suggest?" he asked cautiously.

"I don't know exactly but maybe we could pretend we meant more to each other than just casual friends. Not that I expect you to forego dating whomever you wish. But we could at least talk like we were more involved than we were, or something."

He made a wry face. "I'm sure we could come up with a convincing story. In fact, if we continued to see each other it would minimize any gossip."

Anna giggled softly at his expression. "The mighty confirmed bachelor would have to admit he knows that he's been caught in the baby trap?"

"It's not a trap. A child is a wondrous thing. I'm determined to be there for him or her all its life."

"I know you are," she said softly.

"But there'll be enough kidding once the world hears the truth. I can just imagine what a couple of guys I know are going to say." For years, ever since the divorce, Tanner swore he would never get involved seriously again. Not that the subject had arisen much but when out drinking with some of his longtime friends like Stan and Tad, they'd often gotten into philosophical discussions after a couple of beers. Tanner had been adamant in his noninvolvement stance. He could just imagine the razzing his friends would give him once they discovered he was going to be a father.

Stan would understand, he thought. Stan had stood by when Tanner needed him the most.

For some reason he didn't want to delay

telling his friends. He needed to call his parents as well. And to reassure them that this grandchild wasn't going to disappear after they grew to love it.

When dinner was finished Anna gathered their plates and took them into the little kitchen. She began to run water over them when Tanner appeared carrying the empty cartons of food. He collapsed them and put them in the trash. Then he went to stand by her as she washed the few dishes.

Tanner was attracted to Anna. If he had not discovered she worked for Drysdale Electronic, they probably would have continued dating. She was one of the easiest women he had ever known to be around. Attractive, intelligent and offering a serenity that was usually missing in his life. And no pressure to make a lifelong commitment.

"You don't have to wait in here. I'll only be a minute or two," she said.

He moved even closer until his arm touched hers.

"Maybe I want to be here with you." He leaned a few inches that separated them and kissed her cheek.

"Don't do that," she said sharply, turning to glare at him. Her face was mere inches away. Without further ado he leaned forward and captured her lips with his.

For a moment she held herself stiffly, then

seemed to melt into his embrace. Gently he turned her into his arms his mouth reveling in hers. She was so sweet and soft and warm. He felt her arms creep up around his neck and hold on. Her mouth opened to his and Tanner deepened the kiss. He wanted to recapture the feelings that they had before.

He knew their arrangement was not for forever. Anna deserved to have a family where the husband loved her and her children adored her. That wasn't him.

But he still wanted all that Anna would give. Her hands were damp, he could feel a trickle of water down his neck but he was too caught up in the embrace to care. His palms moved over her back as he pressed her closer. Anna made a small sound of protest. Tanner raised his head and gazed down into her eyes.

"We shouldn't be doing this," she said breathlessly.

"I figured we needed some practice to be sure we can pull off the pretense once we've told the world," he said. It was a lame excuse, but he wanted to kiss her, feel her soft body pressed against his. If she bought the reasoning, why not?

Anna shook her head. "Nice try," she said. "But that's one area in which you need no practice."

Tanner smiled and slowly released her. "I'm interested in your idea of showing we are romantically involved. If kisses are off-limits what do you suggest?"

Anna dropped her hands and looked at him warily. "I didn't say kisses per se were off-limits. But that you do not need practice. And I don't need the temptation."

Tanner raised an eyebrow. "Temptation?"

She stepped back, bumping against the edge of the sink. "You have to know from the summer how attractive I find you. And kisses like that will lead us right back into the bedroom. Which is what got us into this predicament in the first place."

He framed her face with his palms. "It was a special night for me as I hope it was for you as well. I'll be honest, there's no way I can keep my hands off you if we spend a lot of time together. But only if you are a willing participant."

She reached her hands up and encircled his wrists, not moving away, not moving closer. Gazing steadily into his eyes she nodded slowly. "I would be willing."

Tanner almost groaned. He wanted her now. He knew there was no taking her to bed tonight. Could they work back to the level of confidence they'd had last summer? Trusting each other, wanting each other? He hoped so.

"I'm going to head out. I'll see you at the office

tomorrow," he said. She talked about temptation, but he was as tempted as ever being with her.

He pulled her close and pressed his mouth against hers, releasing her before she could respond. With a flick of a finger gently against her cheek, he turned and left before he made an even bigger fool of himself over her.

Anna heard the front door close. She could not move. Bemused, she felt tears begin to fill her eyes. If things had been different, she could have fallen in love with Tanner Forsythe.

Anna arrived at work early Monday morning. She'd rested as much as she could during the weekend, but she was still tired. Staying awake long into the night thinking about Tanner had not helped.

She wondered how the future would unfold. She hadn't a clue how his being a part of her private life would impact their working relationship.

Which would fall apart if she didn't do her job. Turning her attention to the work at hand she returned the call of a long-term client, and threw herself into her tasks.

She was going to make this pregnancy proceed the way she wanted. She may only have one baby and she wanted everything about it to be perfect.

Shortly after nine, Ellie called about a meeting

Tanner would be holding at ten. "He's introducing a couple of new men he's hired. Sparks will fly in marketing," she warned.

Anna knew there would be changes with a new man at the helm, but somehow she thought she'd know about them before others. She couldn't believe she thought she had the inside line to Tanner Forsythe. He hadn't become the head of such a large company at a young age by blabbing his business far and wide.

Promptly at ten Anna entered the large conference room. There were only four other directors—not the large group there had been on the day Mr. Taylor retired.

She nodded at the others and took a seat opposite the marketing director. She wondered what changes were coming his way and had Ellie warned him as well.

Tanner entered, two men right behind him. He nodded to the group already seated and waited while the newcomers found seats on the opposite sides of the table.

"I've hired two new directors, with approval of the Board. James Ruston will now head up the Domestic Sales force. His directive is to increase sales twenty-five percent in the next six months. Please give him your full cooperation and assistance so he can achieve that goal."

Everyone looked at the dark-haired man seated on the same side as Anna. He inclined his head slightly.

"I've reviewed the current strategies and will be meeting with the entire sales force in the next week. I want input from everyone, any ideas, no matter how far-fetched they may seem on the surface. I'll decide which to use or ignore," he said. "I look forward to meeting you all. Hope you can help me out."

Tanner waited a beat then looked at the second man. "Al Henning will head up domestic marketing. He comes with a strong background in electronics and knows how to build name recognition." Tanner mentioned the name of the company he formerly worked for—recognizable worldwide.

"Now, I'd like each of the rest of you to introduce yourselves and give these men a bit of background with your area or expertise."

The drill was repeated as it had been when Tanner started, only a few weeks ago.

Once that was complete, Tanner began asking for updates. Bill Stewart's report was incomplete and Tanner called him on it.

"I expect you to have all the information immediately available. How can you run your department if you lack the data necessary to make decisions?" Tanner was uncompromising in his desire for excellence.

Hank Brownson was next with the accounting department's updates. He knew the answers to each question Tanner posed after his brief report. But the stress showed by the perspiration on his forehead by the end of his moment on the hot seat.

"Anna, what's the status of the new move into Italy? Time frames, costs, difficulties perceived?"

Anna was caught unaware. She'd done an analysis for that market a few weeks ago, but nothing had been done. It was one of the ones she'd listed in her paper to Tanner when he first arrived. But he'd said nothing further.

"We plan implementation to begin in January when I'm there to oversee the project," she began.

"Why the delay? Preliminary groundwork could be laid now. You don't have to be there, you're not doing the daily tasks. Brussels isn't in Italy to begin with."

He was right.

"However, Thomas is still in charge. I thought we'd retain the original schedule until he retires."

"We can't go into a holding mode until Thomas decides when he's going to retire. As it stands, he may stay on another six months. I'd like a complete update by next week's meeting—including a time line that starts now."

He questioned her on two other projects, which Anna felt fortunate she could answer. However her responses weren't completely satisfactory. No wonder Hank had been perspiring. She felt flustered and inept. She hadn't felt so ill prepared in many years.

And Tanner cut her no slack. His implacable expression gave no hint that he'd kissed her passionately just two nights ago. Or that they'd made love all night long once upon a time.

When he moved to the next manager, it was all Anna could do not to give a huge sigh of relief. Working for Tanner Forsythe was going to be totally different from working for Mr. Taylor.

The two new men gave their own introductions, giving some of their background and each informing the group about immediate plans.

Anna felt drained when the meeting ended shortly before noon.

She grabbed a bite to eat, took a quick walk around the block, then barricaded herself in her office to get to the tasks assigned. She would give Tanner no cause to fault her work.

It was almost six o'clock when Tanner appeared in her doorway. "Want to grab a bite to eat?"

She looked up from the charts she was working on, startled to see him. For a moment she relived her embarrassment at the morning's meeting. The man standing in front of her looked relaxed, not like the driven businessman of earlier.

"It's past time you left work. And since you have to eat, we might as well eat together," he said easily. His dark eyes took in the stacks of papers, the time line she had up on her computer.

"It's not that late. Anyway, you're a great one to talk—haven't you been here late every night since you started?" She felt uncertain. Was this the man who would chew her out if she failed? Or the father of the baby she carried? Or the fun-loving guy who had spent so much time with her last summer?

Her eyes were drawn to his mouth. Would there be kisses for dessert? Her heart began to beat a bit faster.

"Okay."

Anna closed the file she was working on while trying to surreptitiously find her shoes. She had kicked them off earlier because her feet were swelling. Locating one, she try to stuff her foot into it, but it was a tight fit. She still didn't know where the other one was.

Tanner leaned casually against the doorjamb and watched her, amused. "Having trouble?"

So much for trying to act sophisticated. She frowned at him. "I'm trying to find my shoe." She scooted back her chair and dropped down beneath her desk seeing the errant shoe in the far corner. A moment later she was standing. The shoes felt tight, but she was not going to dinner wearing her cross-trainers.

"All ready," she said brightly. She knew enough of the corporate game to never let her boss know of any problems. If he didn't refer to the morning, she never would!

Most of the other employees had left for the day. There were one or two they encountered on their way to the elevator. When they called out good-nights, Anna smiled and gave a quick glance at Tanner.

"Aren't you worried there'll be talk?" she asked when they waited for the elevator.

"No," he said, virtually ignoring the other employees. Once again Anna felt she was the only person in Tanner's world.

"How far is your doctor's office from here?" Tanner asked when they were seated at the small grill near the office. It was not as crowded as lunchtime and they sat at a table fairly isolated from other diners.

"About a ten-minute drive. I don't have a car. I take taxies."

"I have one, I'll drive. We leave at four-thirty?"

"If you're driving, we can leave later. It's not far and there is parking. Four forty-five?"

How could he talk so easily about their upcoming visit to the doctor. She had a dozen qualms. She was getting in too deep with Tanner. He seemed to be directing this relationship. She wanted some autonomy.

"Have you hired all the people you intend to?" she asked, deliberately changing the subject.

He looked up from the menu he was perusing. "No." He looked back down.

Anna felt put firmly in place. She decided on a light grilled fish and was ready when the waiter took their order.

"Do you know for a fact Thomas is delaying his retirement for another six months?" she asked. Today had been the first she heard of the change, and when she tried to reach Thomas to confirm, it was too late due to the time zone differences.

"Yes."

If he didn't contribute more to the conversation than that, it was going to be a long, quiet meal.

He reached out to take one of her hands, holding it loosely, rubbing his thumb across the back.

"I'm not here to talk about business, Anna. Make an appointment with Ellie tomorrow if you want to know more. Right now, I'm trying to learn more about you and this pregnancy."

"I'm fine. So far."

"You've made mention before that you may not carry the baby to delivery. How serious is it?"

"What do you think? That I'm worrying for nothing?"

"No, I'm still getting used to the idea I could be a father again. I mean, be a father."

"You were Zach's father for a year. He'll always have a place in your heart, won't he?" she said gently.

He shrugged. Anna was touched despite his attempt to brush it off. Most men didn't like emotional scenes. Make that all men.

"I've been thinking about what we're going to do when he arrives," Tanner said.

"He?" she asked.

"Well, it could be a she, I suppose, but for sake of saying something besides it, I'm thinking a little boy."

"Don't all men want a boy?"

"Sure. Or a girl. Mostly I want a healthy child."

"As do I," Anna said, the fear that constantly lurked rearing up until she felt suffocated. She withdrew her hand and took a sip of water, forcing it past the block in her throat. She wanted this baby so bad she was afraid.

"So what did you want to suggest?" she asked a minute later. She concentrated on her breathing, trying to quell the attraction she experienced every time she was near Tanner. Shouldn't she be becoming inoculated?

"We hire a nanny to watch him. She would be able to bring him to my place or live with you at yours. She'd offer stability to the child and make sure he has constant care. No shuffling to day care or having different sitters or housekeepers at each resident."

Anna hadn't thought that far ahead. She would need someone to watch the baby once she returned to work. She'd thought of an au pair—but she'd also thought she'd be in Brussels by then.

"I don't have a big enough apartment to have live-in help. In fact, it'll be crowded with the baby."

"So move. In fact, why not move to an apartment in the same building as mine. Make it a lot easier to share the baby that way."

The man was crazy. Did he think she was made of money? For one moment she almost asked for a raise large enough to cover the cost of living in that high-rise apartment building he called home. That would serve him right.

"It's something to think about," she said slowly.

"Perfect solution," Tanner said.

Perfect for him. She wasn't sure how she would

come out on top. It would cost much more than she was used to spending—at the same time she'd have other costs with a new infant.

"I can have Ellie begin to search—"

"No," she interrupted. "First it's too soon, and second, I'll take care of that aspect myself."

He studied her then nodded.

The waiter brought their meals. Anna deliberately changed the topic to a movie she'd seen with her friend Marianne a few weeks ago. Tanner had not seen it, so she spent more time than was warranted explaining it to him. She wanted to enjoy the evening then to go home and take some time to assimilate all the aspects of the day.

Tuesday afternoon Anna and Tanner once again left together. Because it was prior to closing time, there were lots of people to see. She tried to maintain an aloof, professional air. Maybe everyone would think they were going to some off-site business meeting.

Once in his car, she tried to relax. But the meeting with her doctor only brought anticipated anxiety. Each week she wanted him to give her assurances everything would be all right. He remained steadfast in his cautionary position.

Once in the waiting room, Anna grew amused at the sight of Tanner in a room full of women in various stages of pregnancy. He looked as out of place as a penguin would.

It didn't seem to faze him. He stood with her when she checked in, then found two chairs together and touched the small of her back to show her.

There were smiles from the other women, and a wistful glance from one or two.

Anna didn't want to say a word in such a crowded place. Everyone present could hear everything. The minutes ticked by slowly. She flicked a glance at Tanner. He seemed as relaxed and at ease as if he were in a boardroom.

Finally she was called.

"Your husband can accompany you," the nurse said with a smile at Tanner.

Anna opened her mouth to correct the woman, but Tanner's touch distracted her.

Once in the exam room, the nurse instructed her to disrobe and put on the gown hanging on the back of the door. When she left, Anna looked at Tanner.

He watched her with amusement. "Don't let my being here stop you," he said.

"Turn your back or get out," she said, feeling the flood of heat from the thought of undressing in front of Tanner. She had insisted the lights be off when they'd made love. She was so conscious of the scars that still glistened on her torso. She could not have him see her disrobe!

He stood still for so long she was afraid he wouldn't move, then turned around, gazing at one of the charts on the wall depicting various stages of pregnancy.

Anna turned her back and quickly took off her clothes and donned the gown. It was silly on one hand to be so shy. They'd made love together for heaven's sake. But it had been dark, and they'd been consumed by passion. She hated the scarring and didn't want Tanner to have to see the network of fine lines that crisscrossed her body.

"Okay," she said, sitting on the edge of the exam table.

He turned and sat on the visitor chair.

"We're having this baby together," Tanner said.

"I'm having the baby, you're just along for the ride," she retorted.

The doctor knocked, waited a couple of seconds, then opened the door. Anna smiled nervously.

"Hello, Dr. Orsinger."

"How are we doing today?" he asked. He was surprised to see Tanner.

Anna made introductions.

The doctor began his exam, asking her questions, especially about any pain in the abdomen area. When he was finished, he helped Anna sit back up, then looked at Tanner.

"I'm sure Anna has told you about the high-risk factors of this pregnancy,"

Tanner nodded.

"So far everything is going well. But as the uterus grows, stretches, the constricting scar tissue could interfere with normal development. That's just one aspect. Her age is also a concern— it's unusual to wait so long to become pregnant."

He smiled at Anna. "Not that you waited precisely. Still, things are looking better than I expected. Taper off the antinausea meds and see if you can hold your own without them. Call me at the first sign of abdominal pain or any tearing feeling."

Anna nodded, hugging her happiness to her. Another week, little one, she thought, just another twenty-eight or so to go.

"Anything special she can do to minimize the danger?" Tanner asked.

"Not at this point. If complications arise, we'll deal with them at the time. I'm keeping careful watch. I know how much Anna wants this baby. Stop in at the nurse's station and schedule an ultrasound for next week," he said before bidding her goodbye.

Tanner walked out with the doctor, giving Anna privacy to redress. She quickly put her clothes back on, checked her hair in the mirror and was ready to leave. She was a bit nervous to see Tanner. The examine had been a bit more intimate than she expected. How had Tanner fared? He never gave anything away if he didn't wish to.

Tanner was waiting in the reception area for Anna. He'd asked the doctor several questions after they left her in the exam room. He hadn't liked all the answers. There was a strong possibility Anna couldn't carry the baby. For a moment he felt the same kind of helplessness he'd experienced when Cindy took away Zach. There was nothing he could do.

This was worse, however. They were talking about a child's very life. He wanted to throw money at the situation, buy a guarantee, but of course nature didn't care.

When she came out he joined her at the front desk and checked his BlackBerry to verify he could attend the appointment time for the ultrasound. He'd been with Cindy throughout her pregnancy, but she'd been young and healthy. Suddenly he understood Anna's fears. There had to be something they could do to ensure the baby's safety.

He was quiet as they walked to the car. He opened the door for her and watched her as she slid into the passenger seat. She was still slender. Dressed in her business attire, she looked professional and competent—hiding the anxiety over the pregnancy behind a serene facade.

Leaning in as she buckled her seat belt, he waited until she looked at him. "I have a better understanding about the uncertainty after talking with Dr. Orsinger. You are not to worry. We'll do all we can."

She studied his face for a few seconds, then said, "Easier said than done, Tanner. Will you not worry?"

He couldn't. He wanted this child. He looked forward to holding him, making plans for the future, teaching him to explore the world and to become an honorable person.

"Dammit, this whole thing sucks," he said, closing the door and going around to the driver's side.

CHAPTER EIGHT

BY THE time Anna was ready to leave Thanksgiving morning in the rental car she was using to drive to her parents place in Stockton, she was a nervous wreck. She and Tanner had not seen much of each other in the days following their visit to the obstetrician. They hadn't really decided what to tell people. She would be doing the first revealing with her family. She knew her parents were happy for the new arrival. Her siblings would be, too, she knew. Still, it was awkward, as Tanner had said.

She'd been focused on her workload, to prove she could hold her own, and the upcoming visit to her parents. She never gave a thought to making plans for after the baby's birth. One step at a time.

Her lease would expire the end of December. Originally she'd planned to give notice the first of December and begin packing for her move to Brussels. Now that had changed. Did she renew for another year? Or consider moving to a vacancy in Tanner's building. It would make things more convenient—if she could afford it.

Arriving in Stockton a couple of hours later, Anna drove straight to her parents' home. The driveway was already full of cars when she arrived. She cut the engine and sat looking at the home for a moment. It was a pretty wooden structure two stories tall, with flower beds on either side of the walkway. Her family had moved into the house when she had been a senior in high school, after the accident. She had gone to college a year later and never really lived in the house after that.

She visited for holidays, but her family liked to visit her—it gave them an excuse to have some time in the city. She loved when they came. They'd talk late into the night, and then explore the city by day.

She got out of the car slowly. Today was the big day, she thought, suddenly feeling sick. At one point she thought it would just be her and her baby. Now her family was getting involved, soon Tanner's parents would be. Having a baby was not a solitary matter.

Only a moment later she reached the front door, but before Anna could open it, the door flew open and her mother greeted her with a warm embrace.

"I'm so glad to see you. You're earlier than we expected. Come in, come in."

Anna's father, Frank, came into the entryway to greet his daughter.

He held her tightly for a long moment. When he stepped back Anna was surprised to see tears in his eyes.

"I'm glad to be home," she said simply.

"And we're glad to have you. And for your news. Whatever happens, honey, we're happy for you. Come on, the rest of the gang is here."

The entire family crowded into the family room. Anna's brother Sam and his wife, Marilyn, were sitting in chairs near the fireplace. Their five-year-old daughter Abby was playing with her cousins Tony and Rebecca. Anna's sister Becky and her husband Paul sat on the sofa in front of a big-screen TV where one of the traditional Thanksgiving Day football games was already underway.

Becky moved over so that Anna could also sit in a good position to see the screen.

"Hi," she said, squeezing her older sister's hand when Anna sat down. "Good to see you."

Anna smiled and returned the greetings, hushing when the men said they couldn't hear the commentator.

It was so good to be home. She studied each member of her family, feeling the love for each that almost overwhelmed her. She wouldn't worry about their reaction; they would rejoice with her.

"I need to check on a few things," Ginny said at the halftime.

Anna took the opportunity to jump up to offer to help. Her mom agreed. Becky joined them in the kitchen so the three of them could talk. Their sister-in-law Marilyn came in a moment later.

"Honestly, I've seen enough football to last the year. And there are all the after season games to get through," she grumbled. "What can I do here to keep busy?"

Under Ginny's direction, they began to get things ready to serve for the main meal. The turkey had been baking all morning. The side dishes were quickly made, dished up. Anna set the table.

Marilyn and Becky began to carry loaded platters and bowls to the table.

Becky told them all about her plans to visit Hawaii the first of the year.

"Paul is dying to go and I want to go while I can still wear a bathing suit and don't look like a whale," she said with a laugh. "Mom and Dad are going to watch the kids, so it'll just be Paul and me and someplace warm. You taking any vacation before spring?" she asked Anna.

Anna shook her head. In the spring she would

be too pregnant to enjoy going anywhere. And by summer, she would have her precious baby.

She hoped.

When they gathered around the dinner table a short time later, Anna gave thanks for her loving family. But her nerves began to betray her. She so hoped they'd be supportive.

By the time dessert was served, everybody has relaxed. They laughed at some comments Becky's daughter made. Then Becky smiled brightly and looked around the table.

"This time next year, there'll be one more," she said. She obviously meant the baby she was carrying.

Anna looked up and involuntarily added. "Make that two more." Heat flushed her face. What had she said? This was not the way she'd planned to tell everyone. Looking around, she saw that all eyes were on her.

"What you mean?" Marilyn asked.

"Are you getting married?" Becky asked, her eyes wide.

Anna glanced at her mother.

Now or never. She took a deep breath. "I'm expecting a baby."

Everyone at the table was dumbfounded. Marilyn looked at Sam. "Didn't you tell me she couldn't have a baby?" she asked.

"Ever since I was in that car crash at age sixteen, all the prognoses doctors have given was I would not be able to get pregnant. But obviously they weren't totally correct. I most definitely am pregnant. The baby's due in June."

The entire group erupted in joyful congratulations. Everyone jumped up from the table to give her a hug and ask dozens of questions—the top one on the list who the father was.

Becky demanded all the details.

Anna laughed. "I'm not giving you all the details," she said. "But this time, when you have your next baby, mine won't be far behind."

"And who is the father?" her brother asked.

"He's a guy I know. Have known for a while."

"Wedding bells?" Marilyn asked.

Anna shook her head.

The question of why no marriage hung unspoken. Husbands and wives exchanged glances, but no one voiced their curiosity. After a moment's pause, the other questions started again. When was it due? Did she know the gender yet? What was she going to name the baby?

Becky began to contribute her experiences, Marilyn joined in. Anna fully expected to be interrogated by her family, but no inquisition was forthcoming. Then Anna knew it was going to be all right.

* * *

By the time Anna left the home on Sunday, she was feeling more confident about the future. At one point during the weekend, her mother had asked if things had changed between Anna and Tanner. Anna had only replied, somewhat.

Her parents expressed interest in meeting Tanner. As had her sister and brother. Anna invited them up one weekend before Christmas. They could all meet for dinner.

She felt a neutral location, like a crowded restaurant where everyone had to be polite, would be the best bet.

Tanner called that night.

"How did it go?" he asked.

"I told them on Thursday. By the time I left, it was old news. They are happy for a new addition to the family. They want to meet you."

"I told my parents yesterday. They're concerned and are flying down next weekend."

Anna leaned back on her sofa, surprised at the news. She thought she'd have more time to prepare for meeting Tanner's parents.

What would they be like?

"So I told them we'd meet them on Saturday. That work for you?"

"Yes." What choice did she have? The longer she delayed, the harder it would be.

"What did you do for Thanksgiving?" Anna asked to take her mind off the impending visit.

"Worked most of the time. Got a lot done at the office with the phones quiet."

"There's more to life than work," she said, wondering if she should have included him in her own weekend plans. How sad to spend a major holiday alone, working.

"That's not how I expect to spend my holidays once the baby is here," he said.

She remembered the agreement they had, alternating holidays with the child. She already regretted agreeing to the arrangement. How could she celebrate any holiday without her baby?

Sometimes in the night she thought about how cold it all seemed. She had long ago gotten over Jason. But she still remembered the excitement of being in love. Of wanting to be with that special person. Would she ever find that? And if she did, would that man mind raising another man's child?

How would Tanner react to her marrying someone? It would probably bring back the past in a vivid manner. Only she was not like Cindy had been. She would never keep his child from him.

The simplest thing would be to marry Tanner. But she refused to let herself fall in love with him. He'd been clear he wasn't going to risk marriage again, despite his halfhearted proposal. She enjoyed being with him, but she held part of herself aloof. If anything happened to their baby, he would be free of any commitment.

That would leave Brussels. She had to keep that in mind. But that dream was fading. Mostly she thought about her baby and the joy of being a mother.

When the conversation wound down, she prepared to say goodbye.

"I'll pick you up around eleven on Saturday. I thought lunch would be easier to deal with than dinner. Don't be intimidated by my father."

Anna frowned. "Is he intimidating?"

"He's a judge and can be extremely intimidating. Works well in court. Just keep in mind that you and I are in charge of our future, not my father."

"Great, sounds like a wonderful time will be had by all. My family wants to meet the daddy of my baby. They'll be coming to San Francisco before Christmas. Once they make plans, will you join us? Lunch sounds best."

"Of course. It'll be okay, Anna."

Easy for him to say.

The next Saturday Tanner stood at his bedroom window for a long time after getting dressed, gazing out at the Bay, whitecaps frothing the surface. Obviously windy—a storm was expected in later that night. But the morning promised only blustery weather. He supposed he should be glad it wasn't raining yet. However, he didn't feel much of anything.

His parents, Darlene and Edward Forsythe, were flying in from Seattle around ten. His dad hadn't wanted to be met at the airport. He was renting a car and would drive to the hotel on Union Square. They were to meet at noon at the restaurant in the hotel.

His mother had been thrilled when he told them his news. His dad more cautious. He'd cross-examined Tanner on the legal steps he'd taken to ensure he would be a part of this child's life.

What surprised Tanner most was how excited he was for this child. He wouldn't lose touch with this baby as he had with Zach. He had parental rights this time around. But the doubts would not go away completely. Legally he had made arrangements to be a part of the baby's life. He acknowledged it was his. They had agreed to an informal shared arrangement. But if Anna moved to Brussels, he would be relegated to a couple-of-times-a-year dad. He hated the thought.

Could he force her to remain in San Francisco? Give the position to someone else?

It would be unfair to Anna after the loyal years

of service she'd given Drysdale. But this was more important. He was considering the future with his son or daughter. And against that, Anna's job came a distant second.

Anna lay in bed, gazing up at the ceiling. Today she was meeting her baby's other set of grandparents. They had been as astonished to learn the news as her family had been. She hoped they'd become happy about it once the shock passed. It was after ten. She should get up. Instead she felt listless and lethargic. She turned her head slightly and gazed out the window. The sky was gray, overcast. She stared at the high-rise buildings nearby. She had too much to do to lie in bed. Yet she wanted some time to herself. With the demands of work, and now having to deal with Tanner's parents, she didn't feel she had a moment to herself.

When did the time come to dream, to wonder? What would the baby be like? Would it be a boy or a girl? She tried to picture a tiny infant cuddled against her breast. She needed a rocking chair. She loved rocking Becky's babies.

She should think of furnishings, color schemes, names. Until Tanner had insisted on inserting himself into the equation, she had been starting with ideas of being on her own and taking the posting in Brussels.

Now everything was different. If she remained in San Francisco for longer, she would need a new apartment—one with room for a baby. She would start planning child care when her family leave period drew to an end. She longed to spend every moment with this child she could after it was born.

She felt a sharp twinge in her stomach and her eyes widened. She held her breath. Her heart pounded. Endless seconds ticked by. Slowly she relaxed when nothing further happened. She rubbed her tummy gently. Should she call the doctor on one twinge? He'd told her what to expect. But she'd been hoping nothing would happen. Was one random pain worth reporting?

"Hang in there, little one," she said. "You still have a long way to go before you can live on your own."

If nothing else happened, she'd wait until Tuesday to discuss with Dr. Orsinger. But one more and she would be on the phone instantly.

Anna thought about the bare bone facts Tanner had given her about his parents. His father was a judge in Portland. His mother sat on several charity committees and did extensive volunteer work but did not hold a job outside the home. Tanner was an only child.

Anna wondered what she'd talk about to

Tanner's parents. She'd find out soon enough. Reluctantly she rose and prepared to face the day.

Anna caught a cab to the hotel where she was meeting the Forsythes. She wished she'd come up with some excuse to avoid meeting them. But at some point she'd have to. They were the baby's grandparents and she could not deny her baby a chance to know all its relatives. She hoped whatever her relationship became with Tanner's parents, that they'd love this baby.

Tanner stood near the large glass doors that led into the hotel lobby. One of the more exclusive ones in downtown, it had several excellent restaurants.

He came outside to meet her as she got out of the cab.

"Are they here?" she asked.

"Waiting in the restaurant. Ready?"

"As I'll ever be."

"You doing okay?"

She debated telling him about the twinge earlier, but it proved to be so minor it wasn't worth the telling. "Just peachy," she said, wishing she didn't feel nervous. Trying to think of them as clients, she drew on her years of experience dealing with strangers to get her through the meal.

Anna recognized Tanner's father the instant

she saw him. His son favored him. Edward Forsythe's hair was graying, but he was trim and fit and carried an air of authority that she was used to seeing on Tanner.

Introductions were made and Anna and Tanner joined them at the table.

"Our son told us about the pregnancy," Edward said without any preamble. He looked at her with a piercing glare. "We plan to make sure we have ample contact with this grandchild."

"Edward," his wife said gently, resting her hand on his arm. She smiled at Anna.

"I understand this is your first baby."

Anna nodded. "That's right."

"Tanner assures us it's his. He should know, but I'd feel better with DNA testing," Edward said.

"Honey, this is not a court of law. I'm sure Tanner and Anna know if it's his baby."

"Like with Cindy?"

The comment stopped Darlene cold. She looked at Tanner.

"It's mine, Mom. And we've already taken steps to make sure you'll have your fair share of spoiling."

A waiter came to take their orders. Anna was grateful for the reprieve. From the unsettling looks by Tanner's parents, she could tell they were not happy with the situation. Nothing she could do about that. She felt slightly queasy, however, and hoped she'd make it through the meal.

"I understand you work for Tanner," Edward said after their orders had been placed.

"I do now. I did not when we were dating."

"You're not seeing each other now?" Darlene asked.

"We're seeing each other." Tanner flicked Anna a quick glance.

She kept quiet. If he wanted his parents to think there was still a close alliance between them, it wasn't up to her to contradict him in public. But he could have clued her in prior to their meeting.

"Living together?" Edward asked.

Anna was startled at that. "No," she replied quickly. Maybe she should set the record straight.

"Actually we're discussing different options for when the baby comes," Tanner said. "We'll let you know when we decide what we're going to do."

"When is the baby due?" Darlene asked.

"In early June," Anna said.

The discussion centered on the coming arrival until their meal was served. Edward then asked Tanner how the new position was going and the topic moved to Drysdale Electronics. Anna was happy enough to let the conversation swirl around her. She still didn't feel very well. She had an achy feeling low in her stomach and still felt queasy. She did not like this aspect of pregnancy. Finally she stopped eating, sipping her water. She'd love to have the meal over and be on her way home.

"Are you planning to keep working after the baby comes?" Darlene asked at one point.

"Yes. While I'm looking forward to having this baby, I love my job. I've invested a lot of years into this career."

"I always found being a mother satisfying," Darlene said.

"So does my mom," Anna said with a smile, trying not to take Darlene's comment as some kind of criticism. Maybe Anna would feel differently at some point, but right now she couldn't imagine not continuing her career. There was so much she wanted to accomplish.

The longer the meal continued, the more stressed Anna felt. Just when she thought she couldn't take it any longer, the conversation changed. Noises were made about leaving. If she could just hold on a few more moments, she'd jump into a cab and head for home and peace and quiet.

Saying goodbye a short time later, Anna almost breathed a sigh of relief as she headed from the restaurant. Tanner caught up with her.

"I'll ride back with you," he said. He studied her for a moment. "Are you feeling all right?"

"Not so good," she said, walking quickly. She just wanted to get home.

The doorman had a cab waiting and Anna gratefully slipped inside, scooting over so Tanner could also ride.

Once the door was closed and the car pulled away from the curb she relaxed and leaned her head back. He took her hand, surprising her.

"Tired?" he asked, rubbing his thumb across the back of her hand.

"Yes."

The silence stretched out for a moment. Anna was horrified to feel tears filling her eyes. They slid down her cheeks. She turned her head toward the window hoping Tanner wouldn't notice. But he was too astute.

"What's the matter?" he asked. "I know my father can be overbearing, but his bark is worse than his bite. They're trying. This all was a complete surprise to them."

"It wasn't that. They are entitled to know their grandchild. It's just an accumulation of things," she said, reaching up to brush the tears from her eyelashes and cheeks.

Tanner thrust a clean handkerchief into her hand. "Such as?"

She glared at him. "My whole life is changing. And your parents don't like me," she said.

She wiped her eyes again with the handkerchief, wishing she would stop crying. It had to be hormones. Or at least a portion could be due to hormones.

"My parents don't run my life," Tanner said. "My father is a hard man to live up to. We won't be seeing much of them. They live in Portland. And his schedule is hectic enough that they rarely travel. My guess is the next time my mother will be down is when the baby's born. She will love the baby. As to liking you, how can anyone tell after one ninety-minute meeting?"

"And how did they deal with Cindy?"

"They were always cordial."

Anna made a face and leaned back against the cushion and looked out the window at the passing scenery. She recognized the neighborhood. They were almost at her apartment. So his mother was cordial to Cindy. It didn't sound like a very good relationship. And at the time, they'd thought Tanner's wife was part of the family for the long haul. How much less would they give to someone who wasn't even married to their son?

"You made it sound like we have some kind of relationship. Like we might even move in together. They have a totally erroneous idea of what's between us."

"And what is the truth?" he asked. "We have a

lot in common, get on well together and we've made a baby."

"That's because you made it sound like we're in love." What would she do if he leaned over and said he was in love with her? Heat flooded her body at the thought.

"I thought Cindy and I were in love, until I found out she deliberately forced the issue of marriage, letting me believe the baby was mine. If that's love, I don't want anything to do with it."

"Don't worry, this is not a repeat." She dried her eyes as the tears finally stopped. She balled up the soggy handkerchief and continued to gaze out the window for the few minutes remaining of the ride.

"What is it you want, Anna?" he asked in a low voice.

"I don't know. Freedom from worry, I guess. I don't feel well and every time something happens, I'm afraid I'll lose the baby. Then there's the un-certainty about my job and my move to Europe. Nothing is clear-cut like it was a month or two ago. And now I'm expected to have some kind of relationship with people I don't know and who don't seem to even like me. It's so much more complicated than I expected. Normally I can tackle anything, but I'm starting to feel over-whelmed."

Tanner was quiet for a moment, his thumb gently rubbing her skin.

"Focus on the baby and let the rest go," he said at last.

She looked him. "Even your folks."

"It'll all work out in the end. Your sole concern right now should be you and the baby."

Tanner waited while Anna went into her apartment building then directed the driver to take him to his own place. He was seeing his parents that evening, but had the afternoon to himself.

When he climbed out, he glanced around. There were a few buildings between his flat and the Bay but staggered so he still had a good view. The water appeared a steely-gray with whitecaps marching in uniformed regularity. The storm looked as if it was moving in with the gray clouds overhead.

Riding the elevator he wondered what he could do about Anna. He'd never seen her in tears. Hormones he could deal with. He hoped. But he hoped she wasn't going to be plagued with them all through her pregnancy.

Entering his apartment, he noted the difference between his place and hers. He'd been at her home several times. Her furniture, her entire decorating scheme was as different as night and day from his. Hers was colorful, warm and cozy, feminine and inviting.

His minimalistic design with black and white tones was far from warm and cozy. He'd deliberately cultivated the look when he'd had enough money to move to this place. He wanted nothing to show him home and hearth, and all the things he thought he had with Cindy but lost when she left.

Had he gone too far? Would their child find any comfort in his place, or feel more at home with Anna's colorful style?

For the first time he considered how sterile and uninviting it appeared. Black leather sofa, glass and chrome end tables. Even the lamps were of metal and cold. The window was framed with black checkerboard curtains, stylish no doubt, but not for a home, a family. For a moment Tanner wished for warm colors, comfy furnishings and feeling of home.

Was he growing soft? Wanting what he'd once thought he'd had? He'd learned from Cindy. Anna was different. But she wasn't into marriage and making a family. Her sights were on Europe.

He'd offered to marry her and she'd turned him down. Lucky escape.

CHAPTER NINE

SUNDAY afternoon Tanner called Anna. His parents were heading for home. He had a lot to think about after their frank expression of concern. His mom didn't know whether to trust that she'd have a relationship with this child or not. She still missed little Zach, though the boy would be a teenager by now.

"Want to eat Italian?" he asked.

"Dinner out? It's pouring rain."

"You won't melt. I'll pick you up at seven." He hung up before she could refuse.

He still had to figure out how to handle the European position that would open up when Thomas left. He didn't think Anna was going to like his suggestion.

Anna hung up. Tanner had surprised her again. It confused her, and had her wishing to know him even better. Dangerous in the circumstances. She should keep a certain distance or would end up giving into his dictates. Why did he want to see her again so soon? They'd shared lunch with his parents yesterday.

No matter, she was glad to go out. She'd been looking at baby furniture online and her head was spinning. A little adult conversation would go a long way.

The strain of meeting his parents was beginning to fade. She was feeling well and optimistic about the baby. Tonight was just for her.

Tanner still had to meet her family, but it could not be any worse than what she'd gone through yesterday. Tanner would be on the hot seat with that meeting.

When he rang the bell, Anna couldn't quell the flutter of anticipation. She had missed him. She grabbed her jacket. Her wool slacks were warm. The sweater casual, but suitable for a rainy winter's night. She both yearned to show she was pregnant, and was glad she didn't have to go shopping for larger clothes right now.

Her heart skipped a beat when she opened the door. He looked sexy enough for her to forget dinner and invite him in. His hair glistened with raindrops. The jacket he wore was damp on the shoulders, outlining how broad they were. His dark slacks and shirt made him look all the more dangerous.

"Ready?" he asked, letting his gaze drift down over her, sending tingling spurts of pure animal magnetism coursing through her.

"Yes." She put on her jacket, picked up a small purse and headed out.

"Bambino's good?" he asked as they walked out together. It was a restaurant in North Beach that they had eaten at several times.

"Sounds perfect." He had parked in the loading zone in front of the building and hurried her across the wide sidewalk and into the dry car. In only seconds they were splashing through the city streets, traffic light due to the weather.

Anna asked if his parents had gotten off as planned.

"No problems. Weather isn't bad enough to be of concern. My mother likes you," he said.

Anna wrinkled her nose. She looked at Tanner. "I don't want to talk about our parents or work or this baby. For tonight I want to pretend we are the two people we were last summer and just enjoy ourselves."

"Sounds like a plan. How far back last summer do we go?"

"What do you mean?"

"Our first date, or our last?"

She tilted her head and gave him a sultry look. "How about right before our last."

He reached out and took her hand, threading his fingers through hers. "I like the way you think, lady." He raised their linked hands and brushed his lips against her fingers.

For a few hours Anna was able to forget the future and the present, and enjoy Tanner's company. She captured that rare feeling she had when seeing him last September, as if they had a unique connection that made each that one special person for the other.

They caught up as if they hadn't seen each other recently, talking about books, and television shows and plans for the holidays. They carefully avoided any personal topic that would touch on the baby, but twice Anna almost let something slip. Since they were her rules, she had to keep them!

She didn't want the evening to end when dinner was finished. Spending time with Tanner was special. But with the rain, taking a walk was totally impractical.

When the bill was presented, Tanner placed several bills in the leather folder, then looked at her.

"There's a club nearby that has music and dancing. We could go for a while. We'll sit out those dances that might prove too strenuous."

"Sounds like fun." So he didn't want the evening

to end, either. She felt a warmth that had been missing for weeks. For a short time they could re-capture the magic of those weeks they'd shared.

The dancing proved to be fun. Anna was careful not to overdo, but as long as she didn't get too hot or expend too much energy, she would be all right. She felt carefree and happy in a way she hadn't for a long while.

It was late when the band finally took a break. Tanner suggested they leave.

"I have an early morning meeting," he said.

Tomorrow was a workday and she had her own busy schedule.

"I've had a great time," she said as they drove through the almost empty city streets.

The rain was a steady drizzle. The lights re-flected on the puddles and made the scene look like a fairyland.

"I did as well. I've missed you," he said. Once again he held her hand while he drove. He double parked in front of her building.

"I won't come up, just see you to the door," he said.

She opened one of the large glass doors and stepped inside, Tanner right behind her. The bright lobby was deserted. He escorted her to the elevator and pressed the button.

"Thanks again, I really enjoyed the dancing."

For a short time she forgot the worry about the pregnancy, her transfer and how they would cope with the future.

He brushed back her hair and held her head for his kiss. His lips were cool for only a moment. The kiss ignited something in both of them and soon Anna was returning his embrace with enthusiasm.

The ding of the elevator arrival intruded.

"Good night, Anna," he said, giving her a gentle nudge toward the open doors.

She stepped inside and pressed the button for her floor. Her eyes locked with Tanners until the door slid shut. Sighing softly, she leaned against one wall, tired and happy.

Monday morning started hectic. Anna had a stack of mail awaiting her and more messages than she wanted to deal with. Her assistant exclaimed how glad she was to see her arrive a little early since the phone hadn't stopped ringing and it was only eight o'clock. By midmorning, Anna had almost forgotten her weekend.

Around eleven she received an internal call.

"Anna Larkin?"

"Yes."

"This is Phillip McIntyre. If you have a few moments, I'd like to speak with you."

She didn't recognize the name. Was this another newly hired manager? Would Tanner be introducing him at yet another meeting?

"I have some time now, what is it regarding?" she asked.

"Didn't Tanner tell you? I'm your new boss."

Anna was stunned. Tanner was her boss. Or had been when she left work on Friday. What happened?

"I don't understand," she said.

"Today's my first day. I'm trying to meet all the people reporting to me today. I talked to Thomas before he left for the day."

"Tanner Forsythe is my boss," she said slowly. Unless he counted Thomas in Brussels. Technically she reported to the CEO, though her assignment was to assist Thomas.

"Tanner thought it best to have another layer of management. I was hired to head up the European Division. My office is the one Mr. Haselton had. I have some time now if you do."

"I'll be right there."

She rose as if in a trance, alternating between bewilderment at the change and fury toward Tanner for saying nothing to her. How could he let her walk in today without any warning? He knew this was happening—heck, he'd arranged it. He could have told her last week, or as long ago as he'd contacted this man. Or last night when holding her in his arms.

In light of the delightful time they'd spent last evening, Anna felt doubly betrayed.

Anna knew Haselton's old office, Ben had been one of the first to be fired when Tanner took over. When she reached it, she didn't recognize the secretary sitting outside the door.

"I'm Anna Larkin."

"Yes, Miss Larkin, Mr. McIntyre is expecting you," the woman said smoothly. "Go right in."

Anna entered and saw the office had been changed—new furniture, new computer, different layout. Fast work for the man's first day. Or had it been done last week in anticipation of his arrival?

The man who rose when she entered was about forty. His hair was thinning on top, but other than that, he looked fit and energetic.

"Anna Larkin, I'm Phil McIntyre. Have a seat. I've been reviewing things with Thomas in Brussels and with some of the other staff. I'm getting up to speed as fast as I can. I understand you'll be leaving on maternity leave in a few months. Don't want things to fall through the cracks, now do we?"

Tanner had even told him that? No one in the company knew. She bristled. How dare he talk of her personal business before she was ready! She sat on the edge of the indicated chair.

"No." She seethed quietly, waiting.

"So, what can you tell me about the division? I've seen the recent sales results. They look very promising. Maybe we can get an upswing before the end of the next quarter. What problems do you see coming?"

Anna spoke with Phil for a half hour, wary of giving him much information, uncertain exactly what her role in the scheme of things was going to be. As far as she could tell, Tanner had brought him in to replace her. How dare he! He must have planned this for a while. Men like McIntyre didn't instantly leave one job for another. Yet Tanner had never even hinted at such a change. He had as good as told her the job would wait for her.

She could hardly sit still for the anger that grew.

As soon as Phil was finished, she rose and calmly walked out of the office, wanting to hit something!

She headed immediately for Tanner's office. She had a few things to say to him.

But he was not there, already left for a business lunch, Ellie said.

"Are you all right?" she asked Anna.

"Just peachy. Have him call me when he returns, please," she said.

"What's it about?" Ellie asked.

"It's personal," Anna said ominously.

She couldn't eat her own lunch. She went for a walk, then returned and called Teresa. Her friend worked in Human Resources, she'd know what was going on.

"Hey, what's up?" Teresa said.

"Tell me about Philip McIntyre."

"What's to tell? He started this morning. His background is impressive. He and Tanner have been colleagues for a long time from what I hear."

"Did you also hear he's heading up the European Division and that I now report to him?"

"No! What does that mean? And why don't I know that?"

"I have no idea, but he called me in this morning to give me the news. I may kill Tanner when I see him."

"You didn't know in advance?"

"No. And when I went to talk to the new CEO, he'd conveniently left for lunch. I think he planned the entire thing that way. He could have told me what he planned. Is this a demotion?"

"Nothing has come through HR. I don't think it's a demotion. But I don't get it. This is definitely something I should be aware of," Teresa said.

"Phil says it's to add a layer between me and Tanner."

"Oh, and why would he want to do that? I thought he was trying to streamline the organization, not add bureaucracy."

There was nothing to say to that. Anna wasn't going to explain the situation to Teresa just yet. She gave some vague response and said good-bye, then fumed at her desk. If this was the way Tanner thought she should be treated, they had a serious problem.

"Ellie said you wanted to see me," Tanner said from the doorway sometime later.

Anna glared at him, putting down her pen before she threw it at him. "I sure do—about Phillip McIntyre and my demotion."

He came into the office and closed the door behind him. "There was no demotion."

She stood. "I'm so angry I could scream! How could you not tell me what you planned? I'm called into a stranger's office and told I now work for him. That he's been made head of the European Division. Tanner, I was promised that position!"

"It's not practical at the moment. And it's not feasible for you to report directly to me. Not given the current situation."

"You knew about this. You've been planning it. Why didn't you tell me ahead of time? I deserved to know instead of walking into everything cold this morning. You had both days this weekend. I thought we had something special going, instead I get shafted the moment I walk into work this morning."

"I knew you'd be upset," he began.

"You better believe I'm upset. I'm so angry I don't know what to do."

"Calm down. It can't be good for you or the baby."

"I guess that's not good for anyone but you."

"Business and my personal life are two different things," Tanner said.

"Not between us. That's all we have is a business arrangement. How could you not tell me!"

"I don't have to tell you how I run this business." He had that hard edge to his voice.

Anna was not intimidated. She stared at him for a moment, then, deflated, sat back. "Of course you don't. It's my own fault. I thought we had something more than we do." Once again she'd misread the situation.

"So when the baby is born, do I still get Brussels?" she asked, holding herself tightly against an anticipated blow.

"We'll have to discuss that when the time comes. I can't promise to hold a job for almost a year. The market is dynamic. Things change."

"But you did promise." He knew she planned that move. How could he now say differently?

Because it suited him, that's how.

"I'll do what I can." He waited another moment,

but she refused to meet his eyes. When he turned and left, it was all Anna could do to refrain from crying.

She felt totally defeated. The only bright spot in her future was the birth of her child, and even with that there was no guarantee. All the years of work, of study. All the planning in the world didn't make a bit of difference.

She went through the rest of the day on auto-pilot. Promptly at five she left, taking a cab to her apartment.

Once inside she shed her coat and sank down on the sofa. She couldn't believe Tanner had been so ruthless. So different from what she had expected from him.

Could she stand to parent with a man who would be so narrow in his thinking he only saw business and not the ramifications of what he did? He had stopped calling her in September without a word—because it suited him. He had hired a stranger and given him Anna's promised job—because it suited him. The future didn't look as clear as it had. Maybe she should leave now before he broke her heart even more.

The ringing of her cell phone woke Anna. Slowly she looked around. It was dark. She remembered coming home and closing her eyes for just a moment. She was still on the sofa, but had kicked off her shoes and covered her legs with an afghan.

The phone stopped. She fished it out of her purse and looked at the missed call report. Tanner.

She had nothing to say to him. She pressed the number on the cell to retrieve messages. There were three. All were from Tanner. The first two were mild, the last one started with, "Where the hell are you?"

Well, wouldn't he like to know!

She went into the bedroom and changed into warm slacks and a sweater. Preparing a light dinner, she went through the motions of eating, not really tasting anything. Everything was spinning out of control. She'd had her future charted out and now it was all falling apart. She could have a baby and head up the European Division. What if she couldn't make Tanner believe that? Was it time to look for another company?

Tanner tried Anna's number again. He had called Ellie to get Peggy's phone number, then called Anna's secretary to see if she knew anything about Anna's plans for the evening. He'd called two friends he'd met last summer, but neither had seen her recently, much less this evening.

He had called her cell several times, growing more worried by the moment. Where was she?

He tossed the phone on the table when she didn't answer. He'd already left several messages. She was undoubtably ignoring him. Maybe he'd drive over there and make sure she was all right.

Grabbing a jacket, he headed out. Why wouldn't she be all right? If something was wrong, he'd be the first person she contacted. She knew he was as worried about her pregnancy as she was. Couldn't she see he was trying to make things easier for her—not to worry about the job in Brussels or escalating work demands at a time when she should be slowing down.

He reached her apartment in less than fifteen minutes.

Guilt played around the edges of his emotions. He should have told her what he planned. But he hadn't wanted to end the accord they'd begun to build. He knew she'd be angry. Once she thought about it, he hoped she'd calm down and see it was the only move he could make.

He was in the right and one day she'd acknowledge it. She might not carry the baby to term. Where did that leave him? Worried about her when she wasn't with him. Delighted in the thought of another child, he had the means to make a difference this time. If Anna proved difficult, he'd bring all his resources to bear to make sure he had an active role in his baby's life. Anna would make a wonderful mother. But the truth was, she'd have been content to have the baby, move to Brussels and exclude Tanner.

If he hadn't stopped seeing her abruptly last summer, would that have made a difference? Maybe he could have handled the McIntyre situation differently.

What could he do for damage control?

In only moments he stood outside her door. He rang the bell. He heard movement, but the door didn't open. He didn't need this.

"Open up, Anna. I know you're in there. I just want to make sure you are all right."

A moment later she opened the door and stood to block his way.

"I was worried about you," he said. He would not go on the defensive. He would state his side rationally and listen to hers.

"I don't know why," she said. "You are not my keeper."

"I called Peggy—she said you'd left at five. I didn't know where you were, what you were doing."

"You called Peggy?"

"What did you expect me to do? I thought you were home but you weren't answering your phone. I thought maybe you had an appointment I didn't know about or something. Secretaries know what their bosses are up to. Only Peggy thought you'd gone straight home. I got worried when you didn't answer. What if you'd fallen or something."

"I'm fine. Am I supposed to keep my boss apprised of my whereabouts 24/7?"

"Cut it out, Anna. You know I'm not your boss."

"Not anymore. You pulled McIntyre in and never even gave me a hint."

"It was business."

"Come on, Tanner, get real. This is as personal as it gets. I don't want to talk to you until I come to terms with your betrayal."

"My—" He stopped. It took major effort to squelch the anger. He took a deep breath.

"I didn't mean for it to seem like a betrayal. I've been thinking of ways to put a layer of management between us since we decided to see each other regularly. It's more prudent."

"From a business point of view, I understand perfectly. From a personal level, you should have told me so I didn't find out from a stranger. Common courtesy dictates you tell me first."

He hung on to his temper with effort. "If you feel so strongly, I apologize. Maybe, I should have told you. But—"

"I don't want to hear any rationale. I accept

your apology. But this better not make any difference to my plans to move to Europe next summer."

"I'm making no promises."

"But you did. You promised I could have that job."

"Wait and see what the future holds. You may wish to stay home with the baby and give up working altogether."

"I doubt it. I've worked long and hard for my position in the company."

"I'm doing what I can do to make things easier for you. You need to reciprocate."

"Then back off. A woman in my condition doesn't need added stress. So promise me the job. Relieve my anxiety."

"If that's what you want, I'll do my best to see you get it," he said.

She frowned. "That's not the promise I want."

"It's the best I can do for now."

"Go away, Tanner." She shut the door in his face.

He spun around. Dammit, a man had a right to run his business the way he saw fit. If she couldn't play with the big boys, she was in the wrong line of work.

CHAPTER TEN

TUESDAY afternoon Anna left work early, killing time until her doctor's appointment. She hadn't reminded Tanner and didn't want him following her. She hoped he couldn't remember where the medical building was if she wasn't there to direct him. Whatever, he did not attend the appointment.

She met a friend for dinner and tried to carry on as if she didn't have the biggest secret in the world to share. But she was holding firm in waiting until a little farther along before telling anyone. If she lost the baby now, she couldn't deal with all the sympathy.

When she arrived at work Wednesday morning there was a stack of invitations on her desk with a note in Tanner's handwriting.

See which we should attend.

Which ones we should attend? If he thought she would accompany him to parties representing the company, he could think again. Take Phil McIntyre.

Anna sorted the invitations almost automatically—putting the must-attends on top. Most of them were for company events to cement relationships for the coming year. When finished, she gathered them up and walked them back to Tanner's office.

"Ellie, Tanner put these on my desk. I've sorted them with the most important on top."

"He wants to see you," Ellie said, already letting Tanner know Anna was there.

"Come in," he said from the door a moment later.

She held out the invitations. "I've sorted them. You're on your own."

"Come in," he repeated, stepping back into the office.

Anna followed, annoyed. "Tanner, I have work to do." She tossed the envelopes on his desk, they fanned out. So much for sorting.

"I want you to go with me. I need a date, why not you?" he said easily.

"Find someone who cares," she said.

"I have. Come with me."

"Why me?" Anna asked.

"You'll know the players, and we'll have a good time together."

"You don't want to mix pleasure and work."

"I need someone who knows the ins and outs of the business, who can also talk to Pacific Rim companies. We want to expand in that area as well. You're the best qualified."

She should stand resolute, but when he put it that way, he was right. McIntyre didn't have the experience with the company. Thomas was in Europe. She was the best qualified. Why hadn't he seen that before hiring McIntyre?

"Come on, Anna. At this season, I think it's okay."

She looked at him, unsure how to take the almost jovial nature of his tone.

"Aren't you worried about gossip?"

"Honey, in another month the entire world will know we made a baby together. Maybe we should start giving hints."

She knew it would be awkward once the news came out.

"I could always be reticent on who the father is," she said.

"I want to shout it from the rooftops."

She felt overwhelmed with his total enthusiasm. What would it be like to be married to a man who was so amazingly pro baby?

"All right, I'll go with you—strictly as a business associate," she said.

"Fine. Which is the first we should attend?"

He moved away from the door and leafed through the pile.

She took the cards from his hand and quickly made sure they were in order. "Temmings in three days—cocktails at the Fairmont right after work, so not so dressy."

Thinking about the parties eased some of her anger at him for not telling her about Phillip McIntyre. Had that been his plan? She wouldn't put it past him. Tanner hadn't risen as high in the corporate world as he had at such a young age without being ruthless and focused. And canny.

As she walked back to her office, her hand brushed instinctively against her stomach where the baby grew. That was the most important thing in her life. If she had to focus on anything—career, personal relationships— all faded against the joy she'd have if she could hold her baby in her arms.

When Anna awoke the next morning it was after seven, she was late. She quickly dressed and skipped breakfast to arrive at work on time.

The only flaw in the day was when Phil asked for a new routine in their reporting structure. It added approval levels to certain ongoing accounts. Anna resented the implication, but there was nothing she could do about it. She hung up and stuck her tongue out at the phone. She still burned when she thought about the change. But it was not worth getting upset over. She had other things to do.

Leaving work she was pleased to find while it was already dark out, the night was clear and cold. She stopped at a stationery story on the way home, delighting in the variety of Christmas cards available. She even stopped by the birth announcement section, perusing the different ones for boys and girls. She felt a slight twinge low in her abdomen. For a moment she froze. It faded and she breathed easier. Maybe she should go on home and get off her feet. She'd mentioned the sporadic pain to the doctor on Tuesday, but he had seen nothing to worry about. Some minor discomfort would be expected; so far the baby sounded healthy.

Cards purchased, she hailed a cab and was soon back at the apartment. She changed into warm casual wear and then prepared herself an omelet for dinner. She addressed her cards, writing short notes in most of them. Next year she would be including the baby's name. It seemed so unreal.

Anna felt another twinge low in her abdomen. For a moment she could hardly breathe. Moving from the table, she went to the sofa and sat so she could pull her legs up close to her chest, wrapping her arms around her knees. This position eased the discomfort. She needed to call the doctor tomorrow. She knew to expect problems, but she wanted some reassurance. She was so afraid she'd lose the baby. As she sat in that position, the pain gradually faded. Almost afraid to move for fear of causing problems, she chanced getting ready for bed.

Sleep was slow in coming. She needed more reassurance than the doctor could give her. There were no guarantees. Please, don't let me lose this precious baby, she prayed.

She called the doctor the next morning and told him about the slight twinges that she experienced. He ordered another sonogram, hoping to spot any probable problem before it could escalate.

Anna didn't tell Tanner. She went alone and got the results. Nonconclusive, according to the doctor. The scarring was obvious. But the baby looked like it was growing normally. He told Anna to make sure she didn't overdo activities.

Only occasionally did she wonder what it would have been like to be twenty-four and healthy with no problems, instead of thirty-eight, high-risk and so longing for a baby she could hardly think of anything else.

The next week flew by. Anna took every opportunity to rest when it came. She and Tanner went out to parties, met friends at restaurants. When she offered to host an event for their company, Tanner vetoed the idea, saying it was too much with her workload and high risk pregnancy.

Anna wished he felt the same about her dealings with Phillip McIntyre. The man was driving her crazy. Anna wondered if that was the plan—frustrate her so much she quit. That would sure solve the Brussels' position, and ensure Tanner's baby stayed in the same city as its father.

But she refused to credit Tanner with being so devious. She didn't discuss the difficulties with him. He wanted to distance himself from her. Didn't want a hint of nepotism rumors around the company. She could deal with this.

Though when Thomas called from Brussels and told her about Phillip claiming one of the new marketing slogans as his own, she saw red! How dare he take credit for her creativity!

She went to see him to discuss the matter. He was attentive and seemed to give serious consideration to her complaint, but then said they were a team and as team leader anything that came up he presented to management. Surely she did the same thing when one of her subordinates came up with a good idea.

"No, actually, I don't. I give credit where it's due. That way when it's time for promotion, everyone knows who has been contributing and who has come up with great ideas," she responded.

"Well, no worries there, Tanner knows what you're capable of," Phillip had said.

She left as frustrated as when she started. But warned at least. Now the challenge was how to circumvent his roadblocks without appearing to be running to Tanner behind his back.

The stress was showing. She lost weight instead of gaining it. She had trouble sleeping at night. Not only because of the tension with Phil.

She still resented the way Tanner had not told her about the change, letting her walk into that situation blind. It proved beyond anything how little he regarded her. She'd been foolish to think they could forge a bond. She was falling in love with a man who didn't care about her at all. How pathetic was that?

Her mother called to postpone their visit to the city. They wanted to meet Tanner, but would wait until after the holiday rush. What was Anna planning for Christmas?

Anna wasn't sure. It was a midweek holiday and she had to work on both days flanking Christmas. If she didn't go home, Anna realized it would be the first Christmas she would spend apart from her family. She'd always enjoyed spending the day with her family, especially once the nieces and nephew came along. Still it would make for a very long day, heavy traffic and the risk of inclement weather.

One Christmas away wouldn't hurt her. Next year she'd be there with her own child.

"It'd just be too much," she said reluctantly telling her mother she couldn't come home.

"I understand. How are you feeling?"

"I'm tired, cranky and sometimes have little pains in my abdomen. I see the doctor regularly. He did another sonogram and everything looked okay, or at least he didn't spot any problem. But there is so much scar tissue, he's not sure how things will work out. I try not to think about that." She knew she should prepare herself for all eventualities, but she was so hoping she'd have this baby.

"Patience, Anna. It'll be fine. We'll call Christmas morning," her mother said before ending the call.

Anna was glad she was home when her mom called and not at work. Tears welled. She dashed them away. One Christmas away from her family wouldn't kill her. She had to focus on the next Christmas when she'd have a little girl or boy to be delighted in.

* * *

Anna was getting ready for yet another party. She had bought a new red dress, for the holidays. Due to not eating well, she was the same size. So far they had only told her family and Tanner's about the pregnancy. No one looking at her tonight would ever suspect.

Tanner arrived just before eight. It wouldn't take them long to get to the restaurant where the dinner was being given.

"I'm ready. I could have met you downstairs," she said, gathering her purse and wrap.

"Good. That's not why I came in. We have to talk." He closed the door and looked at her closely.

Anna found the words ominous.

"About what?" she asked.

"This and that. How are you and Phil doing?"

She wouldn't have gone to Tanner behind her new boss's back, but nothing said she couldn't answer a direct question. She folded her coat over her arm and thought about it for a moment.

"Badly. He takes credit for my work. He doesn't listen half the time and I think it's because he's a guy and I'm a woman. And he reversed some of the strategies Tom and I had put in place a few months ago before they've had time to work." Tanner may not like what he heard, but she wasn't going to lie.

He rubbed his hand across the back of his neck, nodding slowly. "Thomas called me today with almost the same report. He's due to retire in a couple more weeks, now says he isn't going anywhere before I know the full situation. And that there's some assurance you'll be taking over. I couldn't tell him why you can't get there next month. He thinks you've changed your mind."

"We could tell him. He won't blab it around," Anna said. She felt a spark of gratitude for Tom. He wasn't letting her deal with Phil alone. "Let me ask you something. If it had been a different department, would you have handled things differently? I can't believe you arbitrarily bring in managers without discussing it with others impacted by the decision."

Tanner moved closer. He reached out and tilted her face up toward his. "I should have told you before you showed up at work that day. I was wrong. I apologize. Can we get past this?"

"I still want to know how you would have handled a different department," she said.

"The same."

"You rushed it all. And the worst part was you never said a word to me. How do you think I felt finding out like I was some lowly peon who had no right to expect anything else?"

He listened to her, his thumb brushing gently against her cheek.

She knocked his hand away.

"I'm serious here, Tanner. You need to reevaluate this matter."

"I don't want you reporting directly to me."

"So make it worth Thomas's while to stay. We're only talking a few months and then I'll be ready to take over."

"Still be direct reporting."

"But from Brussels. People could hardly think I was influencing you unduly from thousands of miles away."

He put his hands in his trouser pockets. "If I reevaluate the situation and still think Phil is the best man, then what?"

"Then you'll have made an informed decision. Whether I remain or not has to be seen."

That startled him. "Whether you remain or not? What are you talking about?"

"I'm not going to continue to work for that man. He's manipulative and self-centered. He wants all the glory. But what's worse, he doesn't even try to get a handle on things before making blanket changes. We've worked as a team for the European division for more than seven years. A stranger with no experience can't come in and run it without some input from us—which he refuses.

He may have been brilliant where he last worked, but he's going to cause major problems in this division."

Tanner's eyes went hard. "So it's him or you, is that it?"

"Just about."

"See why I didn't want to have you reporting to me? This is exactly what I wanted to avoid—ultimatums."

"Seems to me all your problems would be solved if I quit." Her heart pounded. She had not thought this through. What if he called her on it? Where could she get another job being pregnant? Panic flared. Surely Tanner wasn't her only hope.

He studied her for a long moment. "If I agree to look into the situation with Phil, will you cooperate?"

"I'm giving it a fair shot."

"But if it's not working, I'd prefer to find out before my key players leave."

She said nothing. The more she thought about it, maybe the right move would be to leave. Something to think about—but not right now. They had a party to attend.

As they walked out of the apartment, Tanner caught her hand. "You've lost weight."

"I'm fine."

"What does your doctor say?"

"The same old thing. I'm still at high-risk. Stress is not good for me. So fix this thing with Phil or I'll be stressed to the max."

Arriving at the glittering affair some time later, Anna was delighted to recognize people she knew. It was business and as such she had a duty to mingle and make sure she represented Drysdale to the best of her ability. No one seemed to find it odd that she was with Tanner.

For a little while, she could pretend she and he were involved in the fullest sense of the word. They'd go to parties like this for fun to visit with friends and enjoy themselves. She caught herself looking at Tanner more than was wise. Each time she'd quickly look away and hoped no one else noticed.

Though maybe she should pretend they had a heavy love affair going. It would make it easier when announcing the coming baby.

Despite the enjoyment of the parties, and knowing she'd see Tanner several evenings during the week, Anna was glad when Christmas came and most of the parties were past. There was one more at New Year's Eve. Then it was back to the daily routine.

Anna spent a quiet Christmas at her apartment. She had decorated a small tree, which sat in the window. She knew not many people would be able to see it, but those living in the building across the street could enjoy.

She prepared a small ham with the side dishes her mother usually made.

At three Tanner called.

"Merry Christmas, Anna," he said.

Hearing his voice she shivered. She could listen to him forever. Would he stop in and visit when picking up their child? Or be impatient to be off to the activities he planned?

"Merry Christmas, Tanner."

"I'm surprised to find you home. I thought you'd go to your parents'."

"Are you at home?"

"Yes. I have too much to do to take time off."

"Well, since tomorrow is a workday, I chose to stay, too. It's a long drive for a day. And I wanted to conserve my energy."

"How are you feeling?"

"Fine." Most of the time. She still had twinges of pain. The internal scarring made expansion of the uterus difficult. Every time she felt a sharp pain, she held her breath, hoping her body could continue to cope with the changes.

"It's late notice, I know, but I'd like to take you to dinner."

"I've prepared a dinner." Quickly she reviewed

her menu. There was plenty for two. She'd planned to have leftovers. "Want to come here?"

"Yes. When?"

"Now is fine. It's cooking. I thought to eat around six. There was a Christmas movie I wanted to watch on television later."

"I'll be there soon."

Tanner bought her a gold charm bracelet with a baby carriage on it. The diamond wheels sparkled in the light. She was delighted when she opened the small box.

Thankfully she'd bought him a mystery book by a favorite author. He smiled when he ripped off the paper. "We'll have to take turns reading it," he'd said.

Anna went to get some nibbles before dinner. Tanner walked over to the tree.

"Did you put one up?" she asked when she returned.

"No. Too much trouble for one."

"Do you normally go to your parents' home for the holiday?" She placed the tray of cheese and antipasta on the coffee table and sat on the sofa.

He joined her. "Most of the time. I went home last year."

"What's your favorite memory of Christmas?" she asked.

Tanner told her about the year he got his first bicycle. Then Anna told about hers and soon they were reminiscing about other holidays and how they had differed between an only child and the eldest of three.

They worked together to put the meal on the table. When eating, the easy camaraderie continued. Anna was glad she hadn't gone home. She would have missed this special time with her baby's father.

Tanner enjoyed the meal—both the food and the companionship. At one point, he asked if she did a lot of cooking.

"Not much. I usually get home late and am not in the mood to start preparing anything. Often I eat my main meal at noon. Then sandwiches or a cup of soup suffices. How about you, do you cook?" she replied.

"Not if I can help it. Breakfasts are my specialty. If I don't grab something to eat on the way home from work, I'll make an omelet or something. Not much point in cooking for one."

"Which my mother has trouble relating to. She has always had wonderful dinners for the entire family. Even when we were teenagers and had other activities, we had a rule in our home to be at dinner. Now it's just her and my dad. But she still loves to cook."

Tanner glanced around the apartment. Had Anna picked up her decorating expertise from her mother? He liked it.

Looking back at Anna, he realized he liked her as well. More than he expected. She was unlike Cindy. Not only in personality, but in years of experience, and in finding herself long ago. She had goals and plans and their one night together had changed everything.

Yet he'd never once heard her complain about it. About Phil, yes.

"I spoke with McIntyre on Friday. He's going to ease off a bit. I've known him for years, but never worked with him directly before. He'll be an asset."

Anna showed her skepticism.

"If not, he's history."

"The ruthless businessman."

"I have a short time to show what I can do. I can't afford any screwups."

She sighed softly. "I felt that way. But life has a way of throwing curves."

"Sometimes things happen we don't foresee, but that doesn't make them bad." He had a feeling she was growing more distant. He had offered marriage and she turned him down. He couldn't believe he'd done so. But as he relaxed in her apartment, he realized they could possibly be comfortable together. He enjoyed her company. Was attracted to her in ways he'd never been with another woman. And they had common business interests.

The perfect match.

Yet she'd said no.

Maybe he should try again.

The thought shocked him. He was not planning to marry. He'd done that, been burned badly. He had his own goals and plans. Marriage involved time with a wife, commitments that would take precedence over work.

Wouldn't having a child do that anyway? There'd be school plays and teacher conferences, sports games and birthday parties. He remembered the first and only birthday party he'd spent with Zach. Cindy had insisted on chocolate cake and Zach had smeared it all over, in his hair, on his clothes, and over every inch of his face. The memory brought amusement. And only a small ache.

"What are you smiling about?" Anna asked.

He was surprised to find he could talk about the baby he'd thought was his without the clutching pain in his heart. He told her about that birthday. And other special days with the boy.

"Did you ever try to find him? See if he's all right?" she asked.

"Once. About eight years ago. Couldn't find

any trace of them. I think they moved out of state. It's a big country to try to find anyone in."

"I'm sure he's happy and doing well," she said.

"I hope so. Cindy was a good mother, she just wasn't such a good wife."

Anna would make a good wife. If she made a commitment, she stuck to it to the best of her ability.

Once again he thought about living with Anna. Sharing child care responsibilities, watching their baby develop stage by stage. He wondered what he could offer that would make Anna accept.

After dinner, they took coffee and tea and moved to the sofa.

"Want to watch that movie?" he asked.

"Do you?" She told him the name and looked as if she were trying to gauge his reaction.

"It's a classic. Let's watch it. Unless you'd rather watch alone?"

"No, except expect tears near the end. I always cry."

He was intrigued. She seemed in control all the time. It was an interesting insight—that she cried at movies.

They sat side by side on the sofa, Tanner pulling her close, wrapping his arm around her shoulders. His thigh was against hers. He could feel the heat from her body warming his. Trying to concentrate on the story and not Anna, he was torn. She was too potent. They could have many evenings like this if she'd marry him.

At one of the commercial breaks, he kissed her. By the start of surprise he knew he'd caught her off guard. The thought annoyed him. Why would she think he wasn't still attracted. They'd hit it off instantly last summer.

"This is nice," he said a minute later.

"Mmm," she agreed, a dreamy smile on her face.

"Marry me, Anna."

"What?" She sat upright and looked at him in shock.

"We'd be good together. You need a larger place when the baby comes. I want to be a part of that baby's life, not some weekend dad. We have lots in common."

"Tanner, you asked me once before and I said no. What part of no didn't you understand? I'm not marrying you because we are having a baby."

"Why don't you want to get married? Wouldn't it be easier to have two parents around to watch the child than one?"

"One day I do want to get married. It just takes some getting used to. Ever since Jason I've thought I wouldn't marry. He'd have to be pretty special."

Which put him in his place. He wasn't special enough for Anna.

Tanner rose. "I'm going to head out."

She stood up and looked worried. "Don't leave because I said no."

"You've made it clear now twice that marriage isn't what you want. I'm sorry to be a pest." He lifted his jacket from where he'd left it and walked to the door. Anna was right beside him.

She reached out, touching his arm, as if to hold him in place.

"Marriage isn't something you jump into because there's a baby."

"I've been married, Anna, I know what it entails."

He could tell she wanted to say something, but she bit it back and shook her head sadly. "I'm sorry."

"Thanks for dinner and the book." He wanted to pull her into his arms, kiss her until she changed her mind, then take her to bed and have a new favorite Christmas. But it wasn't going to happen.

"Thank you for the bracelet." She was always polite.

Tanner walked down the stairs, trying to burn off some of his frustration. He had to come to terms with her rejection and still maintain a friendship. No more kisses. The thought almost had him turn around and renegotiate their arrangement. He should have included that in the legal agreement they'd signed.

Maybe once the baby was born, she'd see the advantages.

CHAPTER ELEVEN

"WELL you handled that real well," Anna said to the closed door. Twice now Tanner had asked her to marry him. This time she'd almost said yes. She was falling in love with the infuriating man. Why couldn't he have said anything about his feelings about her? Surely he cared. Or were kisses like his the kind he gave every woman? She hoped not.

And there would probably be no more kisses. She sighed. She wished she'd handled it totally differently.

Or that he had. Why couldn't he have fallen in love with her? She was good enough to have his baby, but not to marry—except for the sake of said baby! She knew she wasn't the type to sweep men off their feet with passion, but she knew he liked her, was love so very far behind?

Heading in to clean up the kitchen, Anna almost doubled over when the sharp pain hit low and hard. She tried to breathe, but clenched her entire body against the pain. Going to her bedroom, she lay down and curled into a ball. The position eased the discomfort. She held her breath again. She could not be miscarrying this precious baby. Should she call the doctor? Telling him at this stage wouldn't help. Nothing could help. She either made it or didn't. But she so wanted her baby. She needed to relax, try to ease the discomfort. Think of something else.

How would life change when the baby was born? She wasn't going to hold on to Tanner. Maybe she'd find someone to fall in love given enough time—once she got over Tanner. She hoped it didn't take as long as it had with Jason. She'd pined for him for years. But she feared getting over Tanner might just be impossible. She loved him far more deeply than she had Jason. And with a child to unite them, she would forever see him, learn about what he was doing, have to stand on the sidelines and keep her feelings secret from the world.

It didn't look good for keeping her job. Maybe a different scene would help.

But not if Tanner insisted on being an active parent in the baby's life. She'd always be around him, always see what she could have had if she'd only said yes.

Without love, however, she would not have been happy.

If she could turn back the clock, would she?

No. Despite it all, she would not change a thing—except maybe Phillip McIntyre's arrival.

Scared, tired and lonely, Anna drifted to sleep.

Friday afternoon Anna was surprised when John Gilbraithe arrived at Drysdale Electronics. He was a customer from the U.K. she and Thomas had worked with for years.

"Hello, Anna," he said.

She looked up and smiled widely. "John! I didn't know you were coming here. How are you?" She jumped up and ran around her desk to give him a big hug. They had dated several times when she'd been in London on business a couple of years ago and they remained good friends.

"Flew in to Los Angeles for a conference, then thought I'd take a few days and see your lovely city. So I flew up this morning."

"It's wonderful to see you. Come in, sit down. Tell me what you've been up to lately. I have to say your e-mails are few and far between."

"Like you write frequently. Heard about the change at the top. Things any different?" He sat in one of the visitors chairs and Anna sat beside him. Soon they were chatting away like the old friends they were.

When the phone rang, Anna called to her secretary to answer it.

"I came to see if you're free for lunch or dinner," John said.

"Lunch sounds great. Dinner, too. Which?"

"Both? We've months to catch up on. Thomas is retiring the end of the year, right? You'll be lots closer in Brussels than here."

Anna made a face.

"What? Not happening?" John was always astute.

"It's complicated. I'll tell you over lunch. Let's get out of here before I get caught by someone needing something that can't wait."

She got her purse and coat and was walking out the door when she saw Tanner in the hallway.

He carried a thick folder and was talking with Phil McIntyre. Anna's instinct went on alert. She still didn't trust Phil farther than she could throw him.

The two men looked up as Anna and John walked out of her office.

Introductions were soon made by Anna.

"I was hoping to have a chance to talk with you while I'm here," John told Tanner when he realized who he was.

"Glad to make time. What about lunch today?"

"Ah, Anna and I have made plans. Would sometime this afternoon work?"

Tanner looked at Anna, then back at John. "Around two?"

John nodded. "We should be done by then. What we can't finish we'll discuss at dinner. Ready?"

Anna smiled and avoided Tanner's eyes. She felt as if he watched them all the way to the elevator.

"Who is the man with your new boss?" John asked once they were on the elevator.

"Phil McIntyre is my new boss." She explained as much as she wanted known. John had lots of questions, some about her personally, and others about the company and how she saw it going in the future.

"Tanner is going to do a great job, I think. He's certainly dedicated enough. But I don't like Phil." Anna wouldn't normally dream of speaking so forthrightly with customers, but she and John were more. And she wanted someone to vent with. Who had known her long enough he didn't have any worries about ulterior motives.

When John heard there was an outside possibility she wouldn't get the promotion, he promptly offered her a position with Poindexter, Ltd., his company.

Anna laughed. "Thanks for the offer, but let's see what happens with Drysdale. I've been with them for more than fifteen years." Secretly she was pleased with the offer, however hastily made. Maybe she wouldn't have any difficulty finding another job if she couldn't remain where she was.

Tanner handed Phil the folder and watched as Anna and John went to lunch together. Men and women shared business lunches all the time. It was the way things worked. But there was something more to that relationship.

For a moment he almost called after them, saying he'd join them. But conscious of Phil's gaze, he changed his mind. He'd get to know John better first. See if there was any reason to suspect Anna had an interest in the Englishman.

He went back to his office and asked Ellie to bring him as much information as she had on Poindexter, Ltd. and its representative, John Gilbraithe.

Tanner was ready for him when he showed up at two. They spoke generally for a while, then John asked about the situation in the European office and how it might impact future dealings with his company.

"I don't anticipate anything but better service and faster turnaround," Tanner said.

"Anna says she may not head up the unit. We'd be sorry not to deal with her," John said.

Tanner felt his gut tighten. "What did she say?"

"Only she may not get the promotion when Thomas retires. I offered her a job with Poindexter if that happens."

For a moment Tanner couldn't believe what he heard. He was working to keep Anna in San Francisco and she already had a job offer in London. For a moment he saw his baby six thousand miles away, only to be visited a few times a year. Anger flared. Anna was not taking his child away.

"Actually I'm surprised Anna even would consider such a thing," he said. "We agreed to live close by because of the baby."

John looked perplexed. "What baby?"

"Anna's—and mine," Tanner said.

The other man looked stunned. "She never said a word. I didn't know."

"We haven't told many people." Only family. And Phil when explaining why he was bringing him in. Anna would kill him, he knew it was underhanded. But he couldn't let this man think she was going to move to London. And the sooner he made sure Anna knew that, the better.

"Congratulations," John said. "When is it due?"

"June. We are delighted."

"I'm surprised. I always thought Anna as a career woman first and foremost."

"She is. Mothers can work the same as fathers."

"Sure. Of course. Well, this is a surprise. We were going to dinner tonight, I guess you'll be joining us."

"I'd be delighted," Tanner said. If Anna objected, he'd tell her John had invited him. "As to business, you can remain confident in the dependability of Drysdale Electronics. We will be increasing sales and enhancing customer service. I don't think it will matter who is running the European office, your firm will be in good hands," Tanner said.

They discussed business a little longer, then John rose to leave. "See you at dinner," he said before leaving.

Tanner sat and gazed off into space for a long time once he was alone. Why had he thought Anna would do as he suggested? He'd wanted to tie her closer in marriage, but she'd have none of that. She was bound and determined to get to Europe.

And he was equally fixed on her staying.

Anna went into her room to put on a different sweater to make sure she was warm enough. Thankfully the rain had stopped. It might be cold, but at least it was not wet. She had recommended a restaurant right on the water down at the Embarcadero. The food was excellent as was the service. But it would be breezy by the water and she wanted to keep warm.

John had arrived to take her to dinner. He'd said Tanner would be joining them. And just why was that? Anna wondered.

She ran her brush through her hair. Suddenly a shaft of pain hit her low and hard. She doubled over, almost unable to breathe through the pain. Sinking to her knees, she tried to ease the anguish, but nothing helped. Sharp pain radiated from her lower abdomen relentlessly. She clutched her stomach, rocking with the intensity.

"Oh, no, oh, no, oh, no. Please, don't let me lose this baby," she prayed through gritted teeth. God, it hurt so much!

"Help," she managed to get out, holding her stomach, kneeling on the floor. She couldn't even stand. She tried to breathe through the pain, but nothing was working.

"Anna?" John hurried down the hall and into her room. "Oh my God, what's wrong?"

Expending every effort, she tried to answer him. Fear hampered her movement. She could scarcely breathe. The pain was intense and unrelenting.

Please don't let me lose this baby, she chanted over and over inside her head. "I need help. I think I'm losing my baby. Oh, please, no."

"Hold on. How do I call for help?" John asked, stepping around her and reaching for the phone.

"Dial 911," she said.

She could scarcely listen to John's side of the conversation. The pain was unrelenting. She hadn't even made it to the end of the first trimester, she thought sadly.

Anna began crying with fear. She was going to lose this baby after being so elated. She should have listened to her doctor but every day she carried it was another day of hope. She had not truly believed she'd miscarry after becoming pregnant despite her doctor's warning.

She curled into a ball, easing to her side, holding her legs close.

"Oh, love, it'll be okay," John said a moment later.

"Tell Tanner," she said.

He looked up the number and dialed. "Take it easy, help will be there soon," he said.

Anna nodded, moaning against the pain both physical and in her heart. She'd known it was too good to be true. She'd been told years ago she'd never have a baby. This miracle wasn't going to end happy.

The next few moments were a blur of pain, prayer and regrets. She rocked against the agony in her abdomen. She couldn't focus on anything.

If prayer alone would save her baby, it was a done deal. But it seemed as if nothing would stop the force of nature. The pain was relentless and sharp.

Tanner broke every driving law on the books, as he wove through city traffic, ran red lights and even went the opposite way down a one-way street. He couldn't stop hearing John's British voice giving him the worst news possible.

Tanner had still been on his cell phone when he hit the elevator running. The connection had been broken at that point, but he'd heard enough. He just hoped he made it to Anna's before the ambulance. Would he know where they'd take her?

She'd feared this would happen. The doctor had been clear it was a high-risk pregnancy. But Anna always seemed strong. He thought she'd have her baby—her miracle child. He liked the idea that he'd given her that child.

Turning onto the street, he saw an ambulance parked in front of her building. He slammed to a stop directly behind it and ran.

Mercifully there was an elevator at the lobby. He leaned on the floor button, praying every foot of the way as the elevator shot up. When he reached the right floor, he saw the door to the apartment still opened. In only seconds he was inside and in the bedroom.

His heart chilled at the sight of Anna curled into a ball and holding her stomach. Her tears struck him. Tanner had never felt so scared in his life.

"Thank goodness you're here," John said, kneeling beside Anna, holding her hand. He rose and stepped aside as Tanner moved in.

The two EMT workers had a portable stretcher and were trying to get Anna on it, but she wasn't cooperating. She kept keening, "No, no, I can't lose my baby."

"Hey, sweetheart, it's okay. You hang in there," Tanner said, going to scoop her up. He laid her gently on the transport stretcher, brushed the hair back from her face. Her skin was wet with tears. He felt like crying himself.

"Hold on, okay."

"Tanner?" she said, looking up at him. He'd never seen such desolation.

"Yes, I'm right here. You're going to be okay." He glanced at the EMTs as if for confirmation.

"Sooner we get her transported, sooner we'll know for sure," the woman said. She reached over to connect the strap holding Anna onto the gurney. It was awkward since she was still curled into a ball.

"Tanner, don't let me lose our baby. I never thought I'd have a baby. I want ours so much."

"I do, too, sweetheart. You hold on. We'll get you to a doctor as quick as possible."

"Thanks for getting me," he said to John.

"Glad I was here to help. Scary situation, I don't mind telling you."

"Whatever you did was perfect. I think I broke land speed records getting here." He leaned over to brush the tears from her cheeks. "Hold on, Anna. You'll be all right, keep that thought."

She gave an involuntary moan. "Thanks for coming. I'm scared."

Tanner wished he could take the pain. "Me, too. But I'm here now, sweetheart."

"Let's go," the EMT said snapping the stretcher up and beginning to roll it from the room.

"I want to go," Tanner said.

"Time is of the essence," the woman said, walking along side, holding onto Anna as if offering comfort. "You'll have to follow, the inside's too crowded and we need to be able to have space."

"Where's she going?" Tanner asked.

"Mercy Hospital," the man said as they hurried the stretcher toward the elevator.

Tanner took time to thank John again and grab Anna's purse. He reached the street just as the ambulance was pulling away. His car driver's door was wide-open. Lucky no one had sheared it off. In seconds Tanner began to follow the ambulance as it winded its way to the nearest hospital.

Fortunately there was a parking spot near the emergency room door, which Tanner pulled into. He almost ran to the emergency room lobby.

"Anna Larkin was just brought in with a possible miscarriage."

"She's in exam room three. There's a doctor in with her now," the admitting clerk said. "If I could just have some information."

"Later." Tanner moved to cubicle three, pushed aside the curtain and stepped in.

"I'm the baby's father. Is she going to be all right? She's not going to lose the baby, is she?" he asked, going to Anna's free side and reaching out to grasp her arm. She looked pale, afraid. His heart clutched. He wished he could do something!

"We're still checking things out," the young doctor said with scarcely a glance at Tanner.

For endless moments only the sound of Anna's crying and occasional moan could be heard. The doctor ordered various tests. A nurse took her temperature—it was elevated. Another set of blood work was ordered.

"How far along is she?" the doctor asked at one point.

"About three months."

Anna gripped Tanner's hand. He switched his attention from the doctor back to her.

"Thanks for coming," she whispered.

He leaned closer. "Nothing could have kept me away."

"Now let me see," the doctor said, moving his hands gently across her abdomen.

Anna let out a yelp.

"Hmmm. I don't think you are miscarrying your baby, I think it's appendicitis," the doctor said. "Call the OR and have someone standing by. Let's get the results of that last test, but I'd prep her for surgery."

"What about the baby?" Tanner asked.

"If we get this appendix out before it ruptures, the baby should be fine," the doctor said.

CHAPTER TWELVE

TANNER leaned back in the uncomfortable chair and gazed at the ceiling. Anna had been in surgery for more than two hours. Her doctor had been notified and had shown up, speaking briefly to Tanner before going into the operating room.

He sat at the end of the room watching the wall-mounted television. Two other people were in the waiting room, one reading, another knitting. Time seemed to drag by. He wanted to storm into the operating room and demand some answers. He prayed the surgeon knew what he was doing. And that Anna or the baby would not be harmed.

Reviewing the last few months, he couldn't believe how much of an impact Anna had made on his life. He wanted her safety more than anything. Next to that, he wanted her to have her baby. He'd never known anyone who wanted a child as much as she did.

The hospital was a top-notch facility. Every-thing possible was being done for her.

Why was he so worried? He couldn't get the sight of Anna and her tears from his mind. He'd do anything to keep her from worry about the baby.

Anything but erase her stress, a voice reminded him. Rubbing his hand over his face he glared at the television, not seeing it. He should not have handled McIntyre's hire as he had. And he should stop being a roadblock to her happiness. If she wanted the job in Brussels, he'd give it to her. He'd give her anything to take away the fear of losing her baby.

He wanted her laughing like she had last summer. Planning business coups that would catapult her division to the top. He didn't want her fragile. But that's what she was today. Would she lose the baby? How would she manage if she did?

He couldn't take her pain. He knew what it was like. She had to deliver this baby.

He checked his watch again. He probably should call Anna's parents, but there was no sense worrying them when there was nothing they could do. Still, he flipped open his phone and called Ellie. He'd get their phone number and called them when he knew more to tell.

No sense anyone worrying like he was. What if something happened to that baby? She'd never get over it. He tightened his hands into fists. He wished he could go in and make a difference. He closed million dollar deals without turning an eye. But he was totally helpless in this situation.

Please, God, let the baby live. It means so much to her. More than anything.

It was forty-five interminable minutes later before the surgeon came out to the waiting room.

"Mr. Forsythe?" he said, coming directly to him.

Tanner stood up, walking to meet the doctor.

"How's Anna?" Tanner asked.

"She's doing well. She's being taken to recovery and will be there maybe a half hour or so, until she regains consciousness. Then we'll move her to a surgical ward on floor three. You can see her once she's there."

"And the baby?"

"Also doing well. We were able to also do some exploratory work, upon the request of her regular doctor. Things look better than first thought. I think she'll be fine. Do you have any questions I can answer?"

"When will she be able to go home?"

"In a few days if everything goes well. I suggest you get something to eat and then go to the third floor. It's almost lunchtime and you can beat the rush. Then you'll have all afternoon to spend with your wife."

Tanner shook the man's hand, not correcting his impression.

He'd asked Anna twice to marry him. She refused. The thought struck him that she was wrong. They belonged together. He had been blind not to realize it before. Cindy had done a number on him, but that was a decade or longer ago. He was not the same kid who had married so rashly. And Anna was nothing like Cindy. She was a mature, successful woman who asked for little, but gave much. She gave him happiness and respite from the hectic business roller coaster. For the first time in forever, Tanner wanted to give back.

An hour later Tanner stepped into the quiet room where Anna lay sleeping. The nurse had assured him she was doing as well as could be expected. She had regained consciousness in the recovery room, but once in the regular hospital bed had fallen asleep.

He stepped closer. Her eyes were still swollen from her tears. Her skin looked pale and tight across her bones.

He took her hand, holding it in his. Never wanting to let go.

Her eyelids fluttered and she opened them. Seeing him, she smiled slightly.

"I didn't lose the baby," she said.

"I know. How are you feeling?"

"Like I'm floating. The doctor said the meds he's using won't harm the baby. Otherwise I would have refused them."

"They can do wonders now with medicine." Unable to stop himself, he brushed the hair back from her forehead and rested his against hers.

"I was so scared," he said softly.

"Me, too. I thought for sure I was having a miscarriage. I'm not out of the woods, you know," she said wistfully.

"I know. But they said things are looking better than expected. We'll go through this together, sweetheart. We won't lose our baby."

She blinked back tears. "I wish you could promise that."

"I can promise to be with you wherever you are. I realized the minute that John called to tell me you were in trouble that you are a hundred times more important to me than the baby, or the job, or living in San Francisco. I have been falling in love with you for weeks. Maybe even before we stopped seeing each other."

"What?"

"I'm at fault all around. Do you think you could consider a long-term arrangement, one that only ends when one of us dies in many, many years to come?" he asked.

"Oh, Tanner, you don't have to ask me again. I've said no twice."

"I'm hoping the third time's the charm," he said. "I want you with me, Anna. I can't take this much more. I love you. Please, think about it. Wouldn't it be good to share the good times and bad? You have brought sunshine into my life. Don't take it away."

"You love me?" She looked astonished.

"Is that so hard to believe?"

"You've never given me a hint!"

"Are you crazy? I've been seeing you despite my firm convictions people employed together should not date. I've introduced you to my parents, only the second woman I've done that with. I've asked you to marry me before—twice! What hint aren't you picking up on? I know that what I feel for you is nothing like what I've felt before for anyone. I love you, Anna. Please, be my wife."

A dreamy look came into her eyes. Slowly she began to smile.

"I love you, Tanner. It broke my heart to refuse to marry you. But you never said you loved me. You said it was for the baby."

"Now your heart can stay whole, and you can stay with me. I'll fire Phil. You can go to Brussels if you still want and I'll find something over there. And we'll raise our baby together."

She laughed. "This is not the Tanner I know. But maybe I should get some concessions while you're feeling so magnanimous."

He lifted his head and lowered the side rail, carefully sitting on the edge of the mattress. "I'm open for negotiations."

"If I have this baby, maybe I should stay at home and raise it closer to its grandparents. I could become the perfect CEO's wife, arranging parties and events and seeing to our kids."

"Oh, and are we having more than one?" Tanner asked startled at this abrupt change. She still hadn't said yes.

"If one miracle happens, why not another?"

"I don't see you as the happy homemaker. It worked for our mothers, but you have too much to offer Drysdale Electronics for one thing. Brussels will always be there. But I won't always be the CEO."

"What do you mean?"

"In a few years, I plan to move on to something bigger, more challenging. Maybe I'll try for an international firm headquartered in Europe. We'll be together and you'll have your shot at the division headquarters."

"Or maybe I won't want to by then. But thanks for the thought. I want to hear more about your loving me," she said with a satisfied look in her eyes. "I've loved you since September. I believe I always will."

"That's good, sweetheart, because I think that's about how long I will love you." He leaned over and gently kissed her.

July

Anna stood in the doorway from the kitchen, looking at the chaos in their living room. Little Emily Rose Forsythe had been christened earlier that day. Now the families and friends were celebrating. The party's honored guest was being passed from one adult to another, and thus far had slept through most of the day's events.

Her sister Becky had been there earlier with her new baby boy and her two other children. Sam and Marilyn and Abby were still there, along with Anna's mother and dad. Teresa and some other friends from work were talking near the windows. Tanner's friends congregated near the wet bar.

Anna nodded with satisfaction at how well everything was going. Then she looked back at her daughter. Her heart swelled with joy. She had managed to deliver a healthy little girl. She still couldn't believe it. Emily was starting to get fussy, however, and Anna was about ready to cross the room to get to her when Darlene commandeered the baby.

"My precious granddaughter needs some peace and quiet," she said, heading toward the nursery.

"She needs her grandpa to rock her back to sleep," Edward Forsythe said, rising with more alacrity than Anna had ever seen. He followed his wife.

They had been staying with Anna and Tanner in Tanner's apartment for two days, and the relationship had improved immensely, just as Tanner predicted. It wasn't all due to Emily's birth, either. Once his parents saw how happy he was married to Anna, their attitude had undergone a dramatic change.

She almost laughed as the senior Forsythes went off with the baby.

Tanner joined her from the kitchen.

"I thought you were going to get Emily away from the commotion," he said, encircling her waist and pulling her closer.

"I was, but your parents seem to have taken charge."

"Did I tell you Dad's talking about retiring—and moving to San Francisco?"

"No. Good grief. I mean, we're getting on fine, but to have them living here?"

"I told him we may be moving to Brussels," he murmured, kissing her on the cheek.

Anna laughed at that. "We are not. You know I'm going to stay home with Emily at least for a few months. Why tell them that?"

"To keep us alone in our own city without relatives nearby. Maybe we could interest them in Stockton. That seems a good distance."

"You're lucky my folks have other grandchildren, or they'd be talking about moving here, too."

"On the other hand," Tanner murmured, kissing her again, "think of the opportunities—we could dump the kids with one grandma and grandpa one weekend and the other set the next and have weekends to ourselves."

"And do what?" she asked, flirting back.

"Fortunately for you, Mrs. Forsythe, I am a man of many talents who excels in planning activities. The ones I'm thinking of involve our bed and a closed door."

She giggled again and hugged him. "I love you, Tanner."

He grew instantly serious. "You are the heart of me, Anna. I love you. I could never have the happiness I have without you and our baby. Thank you for giving me the child of my dreams."

"Oh, Tanner, I'm the happy one. I have you, our precious baby and the marriage beyond my dreams," she said before he kissed her again.

* * * * *

Turn the page for a sneak preview
of the first book in the new miniseries
DIAMONDS DOWN UNDER
from Silhouette Desire®,
VOWS & A VENGEFUL GROOM
by Bronwyn Jameson

Available January 2008
(SD #1843)

Silhouette Desire®
Always Powerful, Passionate and Provocative

Kimberley Blackstone didn't notice the waiting horde of media until it was too late. Flashbulbs exploded around her like a New Year's light show. She skidded to a halt, so abruptly her trailing suitcase all but overtook her.

This had to be a case of mistaken identity. Surely. Kimberley hadn't been on the paparazzi hit list for close to a decade, not since she'd estranged herself from her billionaire father and his headline-hungry diamond business.

But no, it was *her* name they called. *Her* face was the focus of a swarm of lenses that circled her like avid hornets. Her heart started to pound with fear-fueled adrenaline.

What did they want?

What was going on?

With a rising sense of bewilderment she scanned the crowd for a clue, and her gaze fastened on a tall, leonine figure forcing his way to the front. A tall, familiar figure. Her head came up in stunned recognition, and their gazes collided across the sea of heads before the cameras erupted with another barrage of flashes, this time right in her exposed face.

Blinded by the flashbulbs—and by the shock of that momentary eye-meet—Kimberley didn't realize his intent until he'd forged his way to her side, possibly by the sheer strength of his personality. She felt his arm wrap around her shoulder, pulling her into the protective shelter of his body, allowing her no time to object. No chance to lift her hands to ward him off.

In the space of a hastily drawn breath, she found herself plastered knee-to-nose against six feet two inches of hard-bodied male.

Ric Perrini.

Her lover for ten torrid weeks, her husband for ten tumultuous days.

Her ex for ten tranquil years.

After all this time, he should not have felt so familiar but, oh dear, he did. She knew the scent of that body and its lean, muscular strength. She knew its heat and its slick power and every response it could draw from hers.

She also recognized the ease with which he'd taken control of the moment and the decisiveness of his deep voice when it rumbled close to her ear. "I have a car waiting outside. Is this your only luggage?"

Kimberley nodded. "I assume you will tell me," she said tightly, "what this welcome party is all about."

"Not while the welcome party is within earshot. No."

Barking a request for the cameramen to stand aside, Perrini took her hand and pulled her into step with his ground-eating stride. Kimberley let him, because he was right, damn his arrogant, Italian-suited hide. Despite the speed with which he whisked her across the airport terminal, she could almost feel the hot breath of the pursuing media on her back.

This was neither the time nor the place for explanations. Inside his car, however, she would get answers.

Now that the initial shock had been blown away—by the haste of their retreat, by the heat of her gathering indignation, by the rush of adrenaline fired by Perrini's presence and the looming verbal battle—her brain was starting to tick over. This had to be her father's doing. And if it was a Howard Blackstone publicity ploy, then it had to be about Blackstone Diamonds, the company that ruled his life.

The knowledge made her chest tighten with a familiar ache of disillusionment.

She'd known her father would be flying in from Sydney for today's opening of the newest in his chain of exclusive, high-end jewelry boutiques. The opulent shopfront sat adjacent to the rival business where Kimberley worked. No coincidence, she thought bitterly, just as it was no co-incidence that Ric Perrini was here in Auckland ushering her to his car.

Perrini was Howard Blackstone's right-hand man, second in command at Blackstone Diamonds, a legacy of his short-lived marriage to the boss's daughter. No doubt her father had sent him to fetch her; the question was *why?*

* * * * *

Get swept away down under with the glitz and glamour of the Blackstone empire as Kimberley tries to determine the real reason behind her "reunion" with Ric....

Look for VOWS & A VENGEFUL GROOM
by Bronwyn Jameson,
in stores January 2008.

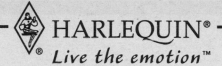

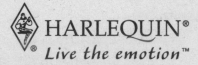

HARLEQUIN®
INTRIGUE®
BREATHTAKING ROMANTIC SUSPENSE

Shared dangers and passions lead to electrifying
romance and heart-stopping suspense!

Every month, you'll meet six new heroes
who are guaranteed to make your spine tingle
and your pulse pound. With them you'll enter
into the exciting world of Harlequin Intrigue—
where your life is on the line
and so is your heart!

THAT'S INTRIGUE—
ROMANTIC SUSPENSE
AT ITS BEST!

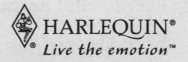

HARLEQUIN®
Live the emotion™

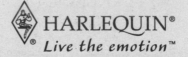

HARLEQUIN®
Presents

The world's bestselling romance series...
The series that brings you your favorite authors,
month after month:

Helen Bianchin...Emma Darcy
Lynne Graham...Penny Jordan
Miranda Lee...Sandra Marton
Anne Mather...Carole Mortimer
Susan Napier...Michelle Reid

and many more uniquely talented authors!

Wealthy, powerful, gorgeous men...
Women who have feelings just like your own...
The stories you love, set in exotic, glamorous locations...

HARLEQUIN®
Presents

Seduction and Passion Guaranteed!

HPDIR104

Harlequin® Historical
Historical Romantic Adventure!

Imagine a time of chivalrous knights and unconventional ladies, roguish rakes and impetuous heiresses, rugged cowboys and spirited frontierswomen—these rich and vivid tales will capture your imagination!

Harlequin Historical . . . they're too good to miss!